D1391776

Lady Catherine's Necklace

ALSO BY JOAN AIKEN

The Wolves Chronicles:
The Wolves of Willoughby Chase
Black Hearts in Battersea
Night Birds on Nantucket
The Stolen Lake
Limbo Lodge
The Cuckoo Tree
Dido and Pa
Is
Cold Shoulder Road
Midwinter Nightingale
The Witch of Clatteringshaws

The Felix Trilogy:
Go Saddle the Sea
Bridle the Wind
The Teeth of the Gale

For further details on these and
other Joan Aiken books, go to:
www.**joanaiken**.com

Lady Catherine's Necklace

JOAN AIKEN

JONATHAN CAPE

LADY CATHERINE'S NECKLACE
A JONATHAN CAPE BOOK 978 0 857 55044 6

Published in Great Britain by Jonathan Cape,
an imprint of Random House Children's Publishers UK
A Random House Group Company

First published by Gollancz in 2000
This edition published 2012

1 3 5 7 9 10 8 6 4 2

Set in Minion

RANDOM HOUSE CHILDREN'S PUBLISHERS UK
61–63 Uxbridge Road, London W5 5SA

www.**randomhousechildrens**.co.uk
www.**totallyrandombooks**.co.uk
www.**randomhouse**.co.uk

Addresses for companies within The Random House Group Limited can be found at: www.**randomhouse**.co.uk/offices.htm

THE RANDOM HOUSE GROUP Limited Reg. No. 954009

A CIP catalogue record for this book is available from the British Library.

Printed and bound in Great Britain by Clays Ltd, St Ives plc

I

The county of Kent, famous for its abundance of flowers and fruits, possesses an equally well-earned reputation for the Siberian severity of its winters, and for the arrival of sudden unwelcome spells of arctic weather even when the season might justify quite other expectations.

A gentleman and lady travelling in a coach along the turnpike road between Canterbury and Ashford, on what had earlier seemed a balmy April day, were abruptly overtaken by such an unlooked-for blizzard. Their horses, blinded by whipping sleet, had veered off the carriageway and dragged the vehicle into a ditch, so that it was half overturned and had suffered some damage. Furthermore, the lady passenger, extracted from the carriage by her companion, who scrambled out first, had the misfortune to slip in the freezing slush as she alighted on the ground.

She let out a sharp cry of distress.

'Oh! Oh dear! My ankle!'

The driver, cursing and wrestling with his team, showed no intention of going to her assistance; but the male traveller, looking around him for other possibilities of succour, appeared greatly relieved to descry through the flying snowflakes, across a swell of rising ground, what looked to be a substantial mansion.

'That will be its lodge, no doubt, at the end of the lane that runs down to the highway,' said he. 'Do you think, my dear, that you can manage to hobble as far as the lodge? The people there, I dare say, may be willing to send up to the great house for help.'

But even as the lady was vehemently protesting that she could not stagger a step, not one single step, and also that she would die sooner than sit herself down on that odiously snow-covered bank, two respectable-looking men, gardeners or gamekeepers, came hastening out of the lane to offer their services. A chair in which to carry the injured lady was speedily provided, and she was transported to the lodge.

This, being very tiny and grossly overpopulated by squalling children and their harassed mother, besides numerous lines of wet, juvenile laundry, proved no great improvement on the situation out of doors, but a servant despatched to the mansion soon returned from it with offers of hospitality and medical advice. The injured lady was carried hither, while her companion remained behind to superintend the removal of his chaise to the nearest farrier.

'What is the name of this place?' enquired the lady, as she was borne up the neatly hedged driveway towards the house, which, on closer inspection, appeared of imposing size and magnificence. It was a large stone building, evidently of recent construction, and remarkably well-endowed with windows.

''Tis Hunsford village here by, ma'am, and yonder house be Rosings Park.'

Her bearer spoke with some surprise, as if everybody might be expected to know this.

'Ah, indeed? I believe I have heard of it. Does it not belong to a Sir Lawrence de Bourgh – some such name?'

'Ay, ma'am, Sir Lewis de Bourgh – but he be dead and gone these fifteen years. 'Tis his lady, Lady Catherine, that you'll be seeing. And her daughter, Miss Anne. A grand fine lady she be, Lady Catherine, surely.'

The grandeur of Lady Catherine's establishment was amply confirmed, as the injured traveller was carried through a spacious entrance hall, handsomely furnished and embellished with marble statuary, across a large, circular antechamber and on into the magnificent salon where Lady Catherine herself was to be seen, seated,

attended by two other ladies, presumably her daughter and her *dame de compagnie.*

Her ladyship did not rise to greet the newcomer, perhaps choosing to delay her welcome until she had established exactly what quality of consideration might be appropriate for this chance arrival.

'So, ma'am,' she remarked, 'I understand that you have suffered a mishap to your carriage? That was unfortunate – or was it carelessness on the part of the driver? Hired coachmen can be abominably reckless. The manner in which they dash about our lanes is often quite disgraceful – I have frequently been obliged to issue a reprimand. Is the damage to your equipage of a serious nature?'

'We hope not, ma'am – a cracked wheel may be the worst of the business. My brother is attending to it. But, your ladyship, allow me to introduce myself, and pray forgive the informality of my arrival in your presence' – for the rescued lady's two carriers had abruptly dumped down her chair in the middle of the carpet and then beat a swift retreat from their mistress's presence. 'I am Priscilla Delaval, and my brother, Mr Ralph Delaval, will be with you shortly to pay his respects. We are immensely grateful to you for your hospitality, and wish to apologize unreservedly for this intrusion on your privacy – indeed, were it not for my injured ankle, we might have made shift—'

'Delaval, eh? Humph,' remarked her ladyship, who appeared a trifle mollified either by the civility of her visitor's manner and apology, or by the name. 'Would that be the Somersetshire Delavals, or the Flintshire branch of the family?'

'Neither, ma'am. We are from Wensleydale.'

'Indeed? You are a very considerable distance from home. How comes it that you are travelling in this part of the country?'

'We are on our way to visit a recently widowed aunt who lives in Salisbury.'

'*Salisbury?* In that case, you are entirely out of your direction,' Lady Catherine commended with disapproval tinged by a certain satisfaction.

Lady Catherine was a tall, massively built woman, well past her first youth, very handsomely attired and adorned with a profusion of impressive jewels. Disapproval appeared to be the predominant expression of her countenance, as evidenced by deeply marked grooves running from nose to mouth, and from her brows upward over her forehead. Her eyes, pouched and heavily lidded, of a muddy, opaque brown, tended to focus on their object in a direct, raking and somewhat discommoding stare.

The visitor, however, remained calm under this hard scrutiny and bore it without dismay. Although at the moment a trifle damp, muddy and dishevelled from the accident, this lady, too, was attired in impeccable correctness in a dark olive travelling costume of silk taffeta pinstriped in yellow, with a fur tippet and hat. Perhaps in her mid-twenties, she could not be called beautiful, but had a countenance enhanced by animation. Her hair – what could be seen under the fur hat – was dark; so were her eyes.

Undisturbed by Lady Catherine's brusque reception of her, Miss Delaval responded with a smile, directed equally at the other two ladies in the chamber, who were both gazing at her with open interest. When she smiled, a dimple was revealed.

'Ah, but you see, ma'am, we could not – at least my brother would not – travel to the southern counties of England without taking in its most beautiful and distinguished ornament, the cathedral and city of Canterbury.'

'Ah. So. You stayed at the Chequers, I presume?'

'No, ma'am. An old servant of my father's, long since retired, supplied us with rooms.'

Lady Catherine nodded her turban slowly as if, while failing to meet with her complete approbation (not having originated in her own suggestion), this course of action might nevertheless pass muster.

'And you have suffered some injury to your foot?'

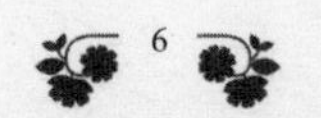

'Yes, ma'am. The sudden snowstorm, you see . . . the icy slush underfoot . . . But I hope that the injury will prove to be a trifling one, only just at present I find myself incapable of walking on that foot.'

'Let the surgeon be sent for directly. Mrs Jenkinson, pray attend to that without delay. And – hmm, yes, have rooms prepared for Miss Delaval and her brother.'

'It is surpassingly kind of you, ma'am; indeed we are most reluctant to trespass on your benevolence,' began Miss Delaval, and Lady Catherine's look suggested that she found herself of a similar opinion; but fortunately at this moment the footman announced, 'Mr Ralph Delaval,' and the gentleman traveller walked into the room. His appearance at once militated in his favour. Like his sister, he could not be termed handsome, but his lively expression and bright, dark eyes, were immediately prepossessing, and his manners, air and travelling costume appeared unostentatious but elegant. He made three rapid, accomplished bows to the ladies of the house.

'Your ladyship – ladies – we are abashed indeed to derange you in this shocking manner. Permit me to introduce myself – Ralph Delaval at your service – and to proffer my most humble apologies.'

It could be seen that Lady Catherine was, in spite of herself, impressed. A wintry smile flickered over her face.

Mrs Jenkinson, flitting agitatedly from the room in obedience to Lady Catherine's order about the surgeon, paused a moment to cast a glance of timid appreciation at the gentleman. And Miss Anne de Bourgh, a pale, dull-looking girl of perhaps seventeen, kept her dim brown eyes fixed on his face throughout the ensuing scene, as if she had seldom in her life encountered so much charm, ease of manner and address combined in one person.

Mr Delaval at once embarked on a lively recital of the difficulties and obstacles by which he had been afflicted in his attempts to find a reliable carpenter or farrier. But here he made a tactical error, for Lady Catherine at once gave him to understand that she would by no means tolerate any disparagement of the abilities and talents to be found in her demesne, and the gentleman was soon made to realize that, had he applied to Rosings House in the first place, all such problems would have been at an end. He acknowledged his error with rueful humour, and succeeded eventually in allaying her displeasure.

'Had we but *known* where we were, and that the two characters I mistook for bearded savages were in fact the leading proponents of the farrier's art and the joiner's craft in the whole county of Kent—'

'Bearded savages, forsooth! Josiah Muddle and Wilfred Verity! Hah!' Lady Catherine emitted what would, in a lesser person, have been a snort. 'For many

years the trusted servitors of the late Sir Lewis de Bourgh and before him of his father Sir Matthew – bearded savages, indeed! Young man, if you are no better a judge of character than that, I advise you to return to your native Wensleydale.'

Mr Delaval excelled himself in protestations and recantations. He had been completely mistaken in his first judgements – had almost immediately seen the error of his view – was now wholly convinced that the two men in question were past masters of their trade and would in the shortest possible time render his chaise entirely fit for the road again. Hastily quitting this inflammable topic, he made a skilful transfer to another more acceptable. He had heard so much from friends and acquaintances of the wonders of Rosings Park, and in particular of its exquisitely laid-out pleasure gardens; now cherished a humble hope that, since Fate had been so capricious as to deposit him and his sister with a broken wheel in the vicinity of these glories, Lady Catherine would of her benevolence and graciousness grant him a glimpse, however brief.

Had either Lady Catherine or her daughter chanced to cast a glance towards Miss Delaval at the moment when her brother was giving voice to these sentiments, they might have observed a flicker of amusement or surprise, quickly suppressed, pass over that lady's

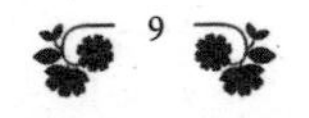

countenance. But, remaining unobserved, she composed herself instantly, and in another moment was displaying no more than a proper degree of interest.

Mr Delaval by now was ingenuously confessing a passionate fondness for gardens, and enumerating the great estates he had already been privileged to visit: Thorpe, Kenilworth, Chatsworth, Beaumain. In some cases, he modestly averred, he had been so fortunate as to be able to make suggestions for improvement, which had been remarkably well received by the titled proprietors and even put into execution.

'Humph!' remarked Lady Catherine. 'You had need to be an enthusiast indeed to wish to inspect even the grounds in Rosings in such conditions as these.'

She cast a dour glance at the great windows, which, at present, displayed no more than a kaleidoscope of grey and fluttering snowflakes. 'And I misdoubt your sister, just now, is in any state to be walking about pleasure gardens.'

'But ma'am, what we are experiencing is no more than a momentary spring shower! Why, in no time at all, I dare swear, we shall see the sun shine again, this little flurry will be over and forgotten, and, I am quite certain, your skilful medical man will be able to make short work of my sister's bruise, or sprain, or whatever it proves to be.'

In fact, at this moment the surgeon himself, a Mr Willis, was announced, and Miss Delaval was carried off by two footmen to a chamber where her injury might be inspected in privacy and propriety. Mrs Jenkinson accompanied them.

When they returned, Mr Willis informed his august patroness that the sprain – for sprain it proved to be – was a tolerably severe one, and that Miss Delaval would be foolish indeed to resume her travels before two or three days at least had gone by.

By this time Lady Catherine was in such charity with the wit, knowledge and good sense of Mr Delaval that she felt not at all averse to having the brother and sister quartered at Rosings for that space of time.

'At this season we do not expect to see many visitors here at Rosings,' she observed to her daughter. 'Since Darcy married that encroaching girl, there is only FitzWilliam who may be looked for to entertain us and keep us in spirits – and until his arrival next week, we are not certain of receiving any but local callers, particularly in such unfavourable weather; our company may be confined to the Collinses.'

She spoke as if such hardship were thoroughly undeserved.

'And with dear Mrs Collins so very close to her time,' pointed out Mrs Jenkinson, 'it is not likely that we shall be seeing any more of her, just at this present.'

Lady Catherine threw her companion a censorious glance, indicating that the topic was an unsuitable one while her daughter Anne was within earshot. But Anne de Bourgh had not attended to what her mother was saying; she had been completely absorbed in a close and apparently critical study of the new arrivals.

At this moment, however, she chanced to turn her gaze to the great window, and remarked in a small, colourless voice:

'Here comes Mr Collins now, Mama, making great haste. He is *walking across the grass.* I wonder that he does not go round by the driveway . . .'

'Oh, mercy!' cried Mrs Jenkinson apprehensively. 'I do hope that nothing has gone amiss with poor dear Mrs Collins.'

Regardless of Lady Catherine's frown of reproof, she ran out into the ante-room, ejaculating as she went:

'Dear Charlotte, poor Charlotte – oh, gracious, what can the matter be?'

Agitated voices were now to be heard from the ante-room. Towards these sounds Lady Catherine directed a look of decided disapprobation and impatience.

'Let me hear what is being said!' she called. 'I must have knowledge of what has occurred!'

Three people hastily entered the room: Mrs Jenkinson returning; a footman, who, in vain, attempted to make himself heard announcing the arrival of Mr Collins; and Mr Collins himself, a tall and portly gentleman, at present scarlet-faced and streaked with wetness from hastening through the wintry weather, who cried out, before he was half through the doorway:

'Oh, your ladyship! Oh, dear Lady Catherine! Such news! Such tidings! I wished to make certain that your ladyship should be the first to receive the intelligence, as would be properly due to your elevated position. So – so as you may see, I have come hastening across the park despite great discomfort and inconvenience resulting from the present unseasonable climatic conditions—'

Not at all impressed by his exclamatory manner, Lady Catherine demanded sharply:

'Well, man, what is it? What has transpired? Come to the point, pray! Is all well with Mrs Collins?'

'Oh, Mrs Collins, yes, yes, matters are going on more or less as they should, or so I am informed by the maid-servants and other females; her sister Maria has arrived from Hertfordshire to bear Charlotte company through the time of travail.'

'Indeed?' Lady Catherine pounced on this item of information with the vigour of a sparrowhawk swooping on a leveret. 'And, pray, why was I not informed that Miss

Lucas was expected so soon? Has she come all the way from Hertfordshire unattended? I cannot in any way bestow my approval on young ladies who travel such distances unescorted. It is wholly improper. I never permit my own daughter, Miss Anne, to ride even as far as Tunbridge Wells without the escort of at least two manservants. I would certainly have expected Sir William Lucas to afford his daughter more care than that.'

'No, no, my lady, indeed, *indeed* you are wholly mistaken. My sister Maria Lucas comes only from London, where she has been visiting a cousin of Sir William, a Mrs Jennings, who, with her accustomed benevolence and solicitude, sent Maria on to us in her own coach with two manservants and a maid. Mrs Jennings is a lady of large fortune, and I assure you she is most attentive to such observances.'

'Well then, why did you not say so, sir?' said Lady Catherine shortly. 'Of course, I remember Miss Lucas perfectly well; she is quite a genteel, pretty-spoken young person. In fact she will be quite welcome here at Rosings House when Mrs Collins can spare her; she will provide company in some degree for Miss Anne de Bourgh. She has a pleasing voice, I recall, and is proficient on the pianoforte, almost as proficient as Miss Anne would have been, had her health permitted her to learn the instrument. But is that *all* you came to tell us, Mr Collins?

Surely there was no occasion to come hasting through the snow just for that?'

'No, no, ma'am, no, your ladyship, that was not it, not at all. What brings me here is the tidings, just half an hour since received by express, that Mr Bennet, my cousin, has died of a sudden seizure. As you are aware, ma'am, his estate, Longbourn Manor, is entailed upon myself; so it is highly requisite that I remove myself to Hertfordshire without the least loss of time, to make an inventory of the property and to attend to various legal matters pursuant upon Mr Bennet's demise. I come therefore to request your gracious permission to set off without delay.'

When she began to understand the reason for Mr Collins's sudden and dramatic arrival through the snow-storm, and his request for leave of absence from his parochial duties, Lady Catherine was not at all pleased.

In vain he pleaded that his curate, Mr Mark Lawson, would provide a tolerable substitute. In vain he pointed out that his wife Charlotte was expected to give birth to her third child very shortly, probably within the next few days, so that the ladies of Rosings House would, in any case, be deprived for a while of her cheerful company . . .

'I am extremely vexed,' said Lady Catherine. 'I was not expecting this at all. Especially when the weather is so disagreeable. It is not convenient, Mr Collins, that you should absent yourself at a time when we are also deprived of the company of Mrs Collins. Consider how shocking it would be if you were obliged to remain away over Easter? No, no; I cannot countenance a departure at such a time, at such a juncture. It will not do at all, not at all.'

Mr Collins wrung his hands beseechingly.

'Mr Lawson is a most capable, most estimable young man,' he pleaded. 'Your ladyship has been gracious enough to approve his sermons on two occasions when my wife returned to visit her parents at Meryton, and I accompanied her—'

'No, Mr Collins. It will not do.'

At this moment Mr Delaval, who, with his sister, had been an involuntary witness to this exchange, cautiously but courteously intervened.

'Pray, your ladyship, forgive my intrusion into such a private matter, but I could not help hearing, and wonder if I may offer a solution to your difficulty? I myself am in minor holy orders, and have not as yet succeeded to any living. May I perhaps be of assistance in this matter? Is it possible that I might replace this gentleman, to whom I have not yet been formally introduced, for a short period?'

Mr Delaval smiled his peculiarly open, engaging smile.

'Humph,' said Lady Catherine, eyeing him thought-

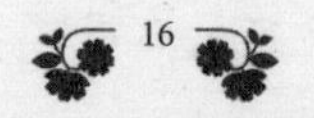

fully. She looked almost ready to be convinced.

Mr Collins, on the contrary, seemed startled almost out of his wits.

'Er – how d'ye do, sir,' he stammered. 'Er – that is to say, my name is Collins, William Collins. I am happy to make your acquaintance, Mr—?'

'Ralph Delaval at your service. By which I mean that I shall be delighted to *be* of service to you, if her ladyship can bring herself to countenance such an arrangement?'

'Humph,' said her ladyship again.

She considered the two men confronting her. The difference between them was marked. Mr Collins, heavy-looking even when younger, had, during the past three or four years, perhaps due to his having partaken of exceedingly handsome and lavish dinners at Rosings House at least twice weekly, become decidedly paunchy, almost corpulent. Quitting his parsonage today in a ferment of excitement at the sudden news of his inheritance, he had neglected to change his costume for the superior apparel he would customarily have donned for an interview with his patroness, and just at present he appeared somewhat seedy and dingy, lacking even the last-minute tweakings and tidyings-up which his wife would have administered, had she not, at the moment when he left the house, been experiencing the first of her labour pains. Whereas Mr Delaval, as had been stated, despite the mishap to his chaise, still appeared remarkably elegant and point-device. His neckcloth was trimly tied and his dark hair, cut by the hand of a master, formed a decided contrast to the untidy strands that fell forward over Mr Collins's damp brow, and his grubby, frayed cravat.

'Well: are you able to preach a respectable sermon, Mr Delaval?' demanded her ladyship.

'So my friends at university assured me, ma'am,' bowed Mr Delaval, 'and *never*, on any occasion, I can assure you, of more than fifteen minutes in length.'

This last statement was almost accompanied by a smile, but sager instincts prevailed and he faced the lady instead with a grave, attentive look, like that of a person who hearkens to the summons of distant angelic voices.

'Well . . . very well,' pronounced her ladyship again, after considerable thought. 'Thanks to this gentleman's most opportune and considerate offer, Mr Collins, I am pleased to allow you one week's leave of absence for the parish. One week! No more. That should be amply sufficient for you to take possession of the Longbourn estate and attend to the necessary legal procedures. (A somewhat paltry and negligible holding, Longbourn, as I recall it, the one time I chanced to pass that way, the park is very small indeed, and the rooms of the house no more than tolerable, with a most inconvenient parlour, facing due west, a thing I abominate.) Sir Lewis did not at all approve of entailing property. It was never thought necessary in either the de Bourgh or the Sherbrine families. Very well, Mr Collins, you may travel to Hertfordshire if you must. One week only, mind – no more!'

At this moment, Mrs Jenkinson tiptoed up to her employer and whispered some words in her ear.

'What is that? What is that? Speak up, my good woman.'

Mr Jenkinson whispered a little louder.

'His wife? What about her? Lying in? Well, as to that, the woman must just manage as best she can. She has her sister, after all. But I cannot approve. All this is exceedingly vexatious. I am decidedly put out.'

Mr Collins retired with more protestations of thanks, and bowing so many times that Miss Delaval, watching him, felt sure he must have given himself a headache.

Lady Catherine, fatigued and harassed by such a succession of events, soon retired to her own suite of apartments, and Mrs Jenkinson, in her usual subdued murmur, instructed a footman to show the two unexpected guests to their chambers, which, by this time, had been made ready to receive them. There would, she whispered, be a collation of cold meats and fruit served later on, in about an hour's time.

Two footmen were ordered to carry Miss Delaval upstairs.

At that, Anne de Bourgh unexpectedly spoke up.

'There used to be a basket-chair,' she said, 'made for my father after he fell ill. See that it is found, Cowden, and placed at the lady's disposal.'

'My dear Miss Anne, how clever of you to think of that!' cried out Mrs Jenkinson, throwing up her hands in astonishment, for Miss Anne de Bourgh practically never bestirred herself on any other person's behalf.

'My sister and I are greatly obliged to you for the thought, Miss de Bourgh,' said Delaval with another of his polished bows. 'Your suggestion is most apropos, and I shall take great pleasure in wheeling Priscilla about during the period of her disability, which I sincerely hope will be a short one.'

'Thank you indeed!' said Miss Delaval to the girl, with her engaging smile. 'A wheelchair gives one so much dignity. One feels absurd indeed, being borne about like a parcel!'

The chair was soon forthcoming, and Miss Delaval was wheeled away in it.

As her brother prepared to follow her, Anne de Bourgh said to him:

'When the snow has melted, I will show you and your sister the way to the pleasure gardens.'

Mrs Jenkinson gazed at her employer's daughter in silent wonder. It was the first time in six months, to her knowledge, that Anne de Bourgh had spoken two consecutive sentences, let alone to a stranger.

II

Charlotte Collins and her sister Maria were up in Charlotte's bedroom, Maria seated in a slipper-chair, anxiously observant of her sister, while Charlotte paced energetically to and fro. Experienced now in childbirth, she knew that this was the best thing to do so long as energy and resolution held out. Maria watched in admiration and apprehension. An unmarried girl, she was not supposed to be so intimately acquainted with the stages of labour as her sister, but she had companioned Charlotte through the latter's two previous confinements, and felt a reasonable degree of confidence in her knowledge of the various developments to be expected in the process of parturition, and how soon it would be necessary to summon Mrs Denny, the housekeeper, and Mrs Hurst, the midwife, who were both at present below stairs drinking tea and sloe gin.

'The house seems most remarkably quiet without William,' Charlotte presently observed. 'It was fortunate indeed that the snow melted in time for him to be able to make his way as far as the stage-coach stop.'

'Do you think he will really be able to accomplish his business at Longbourn within a week?'

'Not for a single minute. It seems entirely improbable,' Charlotte said matter-of-factly. 'He will be obliged to write to Lady Catherine asking for an extension of his leave. All the affairs of an estate cannot be wound up so quickly. But his ownership of Longbourn cannot help but raise him somewhat in Lady Catherine's estimation. An *Esquire* after his name will cause her to use him with a trifle more consideration. I calculate that he may remain away for at least two and a half weeks.'

She spoke as if the prospect of her husband's continued absence from home would be no hardship, and went on:

'But you say that, latterly, Mr Bennet lived at Longbourn alone? So there will not be a great household to disperse?'

'No, certainly; since Mrs Bennet's death and the departure of Kitty, he has spent less and less time in Hertfordshire. Mostly he would be staying in Derbyshire with Elizabeth or Jane.'

'And Mary? Where is she?'

'She has gone to live with Kitty in London. Kitty, you may recall, was married two years ago to some connection of their uncle, Mr Gardner. Do you think, Charlotte, that Mr Collins will wish to give up his living here, and reside at Longbourn? It is a much bigger house, and more comfortable than this one.'

'No, I do not think he will wish to do that,' replied Charlotte with decision. 'He is far too dependent on Lady Catherine's favour and goodwill to wish to sever himself from Rosings. I think he will find a tenant for Longbourn and so augment our income – an increase we shall be glad of, with the enlargement of our family. Mr Willis tells me that this time I am to expect twins.'

'Oh, Charlotte!'

'I shall not mind that at all,' Charlotte said calmly. 'I dare say they will amuse each other. And as soon as they are weaned, I plan to start teaching Lucy and Sam.'

'Are they not rather young for that?'

'Lucy will be four and Sam three; I think children cannot begin learning too early. I shall keep them at home with me. I cannot agree with our mother's practice of boarding children out in some cottage in the village until they are six or seven; by that time they grow shockingly spoiled, pick up all kinds of unsuitable language and also, as often as not, contract some illness which may prove fatal.'

'Good heavens, Charlotte!' said Maria, greatly startled at this rejection of Lady Lucas's well-known tenets of child-rearing.

'Well? Did not two of our brothers take smallpox from the village children and die?'

'Yes, that is true. But then, why are Lucy and Sam boarded out at present?'

'It is only for a week or so, until I am on my feet again. Lady Catherine does not approve of my opinions either,' Charlotte added calmly. 'And Mr Collins, of course, took her side, but on this point I am resolved to be firm and have my way. Why, for that matter, Lady Catherine's own son, Eadred, the elder brother of Anne de Bourgh, contracted a putrid fever while boarded out in Hunsford when there was a typhus epidemic, and died before he was out of short coats. (This was before Mr Collins came to Hunsford.) I am told that Sir Lewis was heartbroken; he died himself shortly afterwards.'

'So Anne de Bourgh once had a brother.'

'She did. I suspect one of the reasons why she is so sickly and lacking in spirit is that both parents greatly favoured the boy (or so I am told), and Anne has always been made to feel inferior. Ever since the boy's death, Lady Catherine has been in the habit of drawing invidious comparisons between the poor girl and her dead brother – "Your brother Eadred would never have done that; your brother Eadred would have been able to learn that easily" – very unfair and guaranteed to make the poor girl even duller and crosser than she is already. I do not think Colonel FitzWilliam is at all anxious to hasten on the match.'

If Charlotte had been looking at her sister just then, she would have noticed Maria turn very pale. But Charlotte was peering between the window curtains and went on: 'Well! I declare, talk of the devil, there is the colonel now! I just this moment saw him ride past. I had understood that he and Lord Luke were not expected until next week. I wonder what brings them so soon? I am sure it is not the colonel's own inclinations. No doubt he comes to escort his uncle. He himself always seems so bored at Rosings.'

Maria's complexion had turned from pale to pink. She now enquired, with tolerable calm:

'It is certain, then? They are to marry? Anne de Bourgh and Colonel FitzWilliam?

'Yes. Lady Catherine told us at New Year that it would be announced at Easter, when they are gone out of mourning for some great-aunt. Anne will have fifty thousand pounds at her majority, you know, very likely more, so it is a fine thing for the colonel. Despite the fact that he is the younger son of the Earl of Wrendale, I understand that he has hardly a feather to fly with. And he may well feel sorry for the poor girl; he is a good-natured, kindly fellow, I have a great regard for him. Anne was half promised to Darcy, you know; or so Lady Catherine thought – at least, she always spoke of the match as if it was an arranged thing. So when Darcy married Elizabeth Bennet, it must have been quite a severe blow to Anne, both to her affections and to her vanity. Perhaps FitzWilliam thinks that marrying her is the least he can do to make amends for his cousin's defection. In any case, both Lady Catherine and her daughter will be delighted to see him.'

'Who is Lord Luke?'

'Lord Luke Sherbrine. He is Lady Catherine's brother, and brother to the Duke of Anglesea. Never married. He lives somewhere up in those northern parts, near to Mr Darcy and Colonel FitzWilliam.'

'Mrs Denny tells me that there are other visitors at Rosings House just now.'

'Yes, a Mr Delaval and his sister. They had a carriage accident. Lady Catherine offered them hospitality, for the lady suffered a sprained ankle. And it turned out a fortunate chance for William, since Mr Delaval, it seems, is in orders and can conduct the services on Sunday.'

'How do you know all this?'

'William met the Delavals before he left. And one of the footmen at Rosings is Mr Denny's brother,' said Charlotte, laughing. 'Not much goes on at the great house that is not immediately reported to us. I heard that the lady and gentleman are very handsome and well mannered.'

'Perhaps Anne de Bourgh will fall in love with the gentleman,' said Maria hopefully.

Charlotte turned and gave her young sister a very earnest, considering look.

'My love, put the colonel out of your head! He is not for you. *You* have not got fifty thousand pounds. And, even if you had, he is promised to poor sickly Anne. You would not be so heartless as to wish to deprive her of her second, perhaps her only, chance— Oh, heavens!'

She put her hand to her side with a sudden gasp.

'Oh, Charlotte! Is it time to fetch Mrs Hurst?'

'Yes, I think you had better do so. And tell her to bring me a cup of hot tea!'

Maria ran for the stairs.

That evening found Colonel FitzWilliam calling at Hunsford parsonage.

His overt purpose was to enquire after Mrs Collins, but when he saw Maria Lucas in the parlour, his face lit up and he momentarily forgot all about his official mission.

The colonel was not a handsome man. But there was something remarkably direct and likeable about his craggy countenance: his face reflected his thoughts and emotions with great fidelity, and just now it was plain that what he felt at the sight of Maria was an incautious delight.

'Miss Maria! I had no idea – nobody told me that you were here at Hunsford!'

'Nor I that you were here, Colonel. I – I had understood that you were expected later, some weeks later . . .'

He said, 'I brought my uncle, Lord Luke Sherbrine. He wished to consult my Aunt Catherine on a matter of family business, and he is becoming too old and frail to travel unescorted all the way from Derbyshire.'

'Lady de Bourgh and her daughter must have been happy to see you.'

He smiled. 'Not so happy to see my uncle, however; the pair of them, for some obscure family reason, have never been the best of friends.'

'And – and Miss Anne de Bourgh?' Maria went on courageously. 'I understand that I am to congratulate you, Colonel, on your forthcoming engagement.'

He became serious in a moment. 'Ah. You have heard. Yes, it is so. My cousin Anne – well, there are strong family interests promoting the alliance; and we younger sons, you know, must be inured to self-denial in matrimonial affairs. Maria – Miss Lucas—' He swallowed and went on after a moment. 'Miss Lucas, I was very wrong, last year – very remiss, in – in allowing my wishes, my personal feelings to make themselves apparent; if – if I have done so and – and given rise to false conclusions, I deeply, deeply repent; I can only humbly crave pardon, and my sense of wrongdoing is all the greater because I know (alas, so well) the kind and candid nature that will be ready to grant that forgiveness—'

He stopped. His gaze was full of urgent appeal.

For a moment, Maria was quite unable to reply. Her throat was tight with tears. She waited for a minute or two, then became able to say lightly:

'Oh, fie, Colonel Fitzwilliam. You make too much of so little! Let us not aspire to any heroics or grand renunciation scenes. Indeed, there is nothing to forgive. The fault, if any fault there be, was equally mine. I should have been more circumspect. 'Twas only a piece of summer foolishness, soon lost in the past. "In folly ripe, in reason rotten", you know!'

Maria gave the colonel what she hoped was a satirical smile, trying not to let her lips tremble.

'No, no!' he exclaimed vehemently. 'You must not say so! For that would deprive me of some treasured,

treasured memories, which will enrich my life to its very final moments, even should I live to be an old, old man. That misty, enchanted evening by the lake when we saw the bats flying . . .'

Maria's involuntary movement of pain, the faint sound of protest that escaped her, fortunately passed unnoticed, for a door near the top of the stairs opened at that moment and the clamorous noise of an infant crying made itself heard, a lusty and importunate howling which immediately engaged the visitor's attention.

'Come, come now, Colonel, you refine too much—' Maria had begun huskily, but, without attending to her, he ejaculated:

'Oh, good heavens! Of course! I was despatched by my Aunt Catherine to make an enquiry after Mrs Collins. But I had my own reasons for wishing to come to this house.' He paused, sighed, then firmly continued: 'I hope from what I hear that all went as it should?'

'Oh, yes,' said Maria with a wan smile. 'Matters fell out just as Mr Willis had predicted. My sister, as well as the two children she has already, is now the mother of twin boys, William and Henry.'

'Oh,' he said rather blankly. 'That must be very – very gratifying for Mr and Mrs Collins. I am sure that my aunt will be full of approval. But I should not detain you any longer. You must wish to be with your sister. She is well? She is not too exhausted?'

'No, fortunately she is very strong, and has the ability to recover quickly from such an experience.'

'Please give her my very warmest congratulations, as well as those of my aunt and cousin. I – I suppose we shall not be seeing you up at the house in the near future – you will prefer to remain at your sister's bedside?' He added rather doubtfully, 'I know that my cousin Anne would wish to solicit the pleasure of your company, if that were at all possible; she has, as I am sure you know, a very strong regard for you' – Maria looked sceptical at this – 'and is eager to renew the pleasure of hearing you play and sing; she sends all kinds of messages to your sister and yourself, and, remembering that there is no piano at the parsonage, wished to assure you that you must feel at liberty to come whenever you choose and make use of the instrument in the music room.'

'That is exceedingly thoughtful and solicitous of Miss Anne. Please convey my warmest gratitude. But, in fact, that – that state of affairs is about to be remedied,' Maria told the colonel quietly. 'On my way here from Hertfordshire I stayed in London for some weeks with a cousin of my father, a Mrs Jennings, who was so kind as to – as to take an interest in my performance. Learning that there was no piano in this establishment, she, with unexampled kindness and generosity, at once hurried off to Broadwood and ordered an instrument to be sent to Mrs Collins's's house. We expect it to arrive very soon and – and then I shall be able to give music lessons to my niece and nephew.'

She smiled faintly.

The colonel looked disappointed but said, 'I am happy to hear that others besides myself place a true value on your talents, even if that means we are to be deprived of the pleasure of hearing you up at Rosings House as often as we would wish . . .'

'Thank you,' Maria murmured, longing for him to go.

And, as if his intuition made contact with hers, he turned with true military alertness, bowed and removed himself from the room.

After he had gone Maria stood still for a moment, staring at her hand, which, when he turned to go, she had raised as if in expectation of its being kissed. But he had not done so. She turned her palm upwards and studied it, but there was no fortune to be found there. Shrugging her shoulders like a horse beset by flies, Maria ran upstairs to her sister's bedroom.

'Well!' she announced. 'That was Colonel Fitz-William, sent by her ladyship to enquire. He brings all kinds of messages.'

Charlotte sighed. 'That means, I suppose, that within

half an hour we shall receive several enormous baskets of parsnips, turnips, carrots, apples, celery and beetroot – we shall be half buried in vegetables for weeks to come. And I must immediately write an effusive letter of thanks – you had better be fetching me a pen and some paper—'

Charlotte broke off from what she was saying and cast a penetrating glance at her younger sister.

Charlotte Collins had never been handsome: she had a square, pink countenance, redeemed by a friendly expression and two clear, intelligent grey eyes. But her young sister was the possessor of decidedly engaging looks. Maria's face was delicately boned, her very red mouth was wide and sensitive, her dark brown hair fell in natural curls and her eyes, large, brilliant and dark-lashed, were a striking shade of grey-green.

'You are looking unusually pretty this evening, Maria, even for you,' remarked Charlotte in her shrewd, down-right manner. 'I do hope and trust that Colonel Fitz-William has not been making love to you?'

'No, *indeed* he has not! I congratulated him on his engagement; I seized the chance of doing so directly he came in, so – so all is understood, the footing on which we stand has been established.'

'You did just as you ought,' approved Charlotte. 'And he?'

'Accepted it as he should. There was no— Anything – anything that might once have been between us is now entirely at an end.'

'Good girl! He is entirely blameworthy, I do not excuse him,' said Charlotte, frowning. 'He should not have allowed matters to proceed . . . as far as they did. Men can be shockingly thoughtless: they do not reflect. Once, there was a Lieutenant Throgmorton, in the militia at Meryton . . .'

Her voice trailed away, and Maria looked up at her sister in surprise.

'Lieutenant Throgmorton? Why, I remember him. Oh Charlotte! Was he – was he ever serious?'

'No, he was not. It was not, with him, a case of money – I had enough of *that* – but breeding, and of that I had not sufficient. Our poor father, with his ironmonger's shop! The knighthood did not serve to screen it. My ten thousand pounds would have done well enough, but not my background, which, together with my lack of looks . . . So, two years later, I was glad enough to take Mr Collins.'

'Oh, Charlotte!' Maria had slid from her low chair on to the floor; she now hid her face in Charlotte's coverlet. 'My heart is broken,' she brought out at length in a strangled voice. 'I can feel it bleeding.'

'Well, you must just set to work and mend it. What of

the handsome gentleman who is at present quartered at Rosings with his sister, Mr Delaval? I received only a very brief description of him from William, who, of course, was entirely concerned with his own affairs. Pray tell me, what did the colonel have to say about the Delavals?'

Maria was obliged to confess: 'They were never mentioned from first to last.'

'Oh, Maria! Shame on you!'

The door opened. Hungry howls accompanied the buxom woman who entered the bedroom with a red-faced, white-wrapped bundle on either arm.

Downstairs, the front doorbell rang loudly.

'That must be Lady Catherine's gift of garden produce,' said Charlotte with a sigh.

'Never you mind about that, ma'am. You just tend to your duty here.'

'I absolutely refuse to have them both at once!'

'Master William first, Master Henry after. 'Twill be t'other way round next time.'

'Hand me William then, Mrs Hurst. Maria, be a love and run down to receive Lady Catherine's vegetable bounty, will you, and say all that is proper.'

But it was the new Broadwood piano from kind Mrs Jennings.

Rosings House was situated at the summit of a gentle

slope of rising land, approached in front by a gravel drive winding in easy stages up the hillside. A belt of woodland protected the pleasure gardens, which lay to the east at the rear of the house. Beyond them, and separated from them by a ha-ha, there extended a large rolling meadow which fell away at first gradually, then more steeply, and was bordered by a wide brook or small river, on the far side of which rose a wooded incline of some abruptness and grandeur. The brook had been dammed in two places to create a large millpond and a fish pond of almost equal size. Rosings Mill was out of sight, a mile away and screened by trees; but at the head of the upper pond, and visible from Rosings House, stood a small, unimpressive building, originally a keeper's cottage but latterly occupied by two men who had been friends of the late Sir Lewis de Bourgh. Both were painters, the elder one of some considerable repute in the world. Formerly, they had lived in London, using the cottage, which they rented from Sir Lewis and had christened Wormwood End, as a holiday retreat. But of late years, due to the older man's decline in health, they had come to spend more and more time in Kent, and had at last given up their house in Hanover Square entirely. Their names were Desmond Finglow and Ambrose Mynges, but since both had the middle name of Thomas, their affectionate friends in the London community of artists, of whom there were many, always referred to them as 'Old Tom' and 'Young Tom', and these nicknames had somehow followed them to the country. Both men, until 'Old Tom' Finglow's health began to decline, had been regular frequenters of the Hopsack Inn in Hunsford village, and they had established friendly terms with local people right across the neighbourhood, from Canterbury to Maidstone and from Faversham to Charing.

'Young Tom' Mynges had an agreeable talent for dashing off small, pleasing sketches of buildings, whether barns, oast houses, cottages or castles, and presenting them to the surprised but gratified owners, who often responded in kind with a load of logs, a basket of cabbages or half a pig. Acquaintances from London frequently came down to visit the two friends, and so, with these and the company of neighbours, the two men enjoyed a larger society, probably, than even in their London days. They received decidedly more visitors than ever crossed the threshold of the great house; for Lady Catherine was decidedly nice in her choice of the company she considered fit to mix with her daughter Anne, who, in consequence, led a dull and lonely existence.

Lady Catherine was not on particularly amiable terms with the two painters. The fact of their friendship with the late Sir Lewis was no recommendation to *her*, and, though she conceded that they were both of her own class – gentlemen – she could not endure their way of life, which she considered insecure and raffish; and she entirely disapproved of the hail-fellow-well-met terms on which they lived with their neighbours, whether gypsies, poachers, magistrates or bishops.

It was therefore by purest accident that Anne de Bourgh had become acquainted with the artists, a circumstance which she had hitherto succeeded in keeping from her mother.

The foundation of their friendship lay some three years back.

At this time, when Anne was sixteen, Mrs Jenkinson had become subject to occasional severe migraines. She did not dare admit this disability to her employer, who displayed scant tolerance of illness unless it was an immediately visible broken limb or bleeding wound. Poor Mrs Jenkinson therefore habitually crept about her duties, enduring the misery of the migraine as best she could. But on one occasion when Lady Catherine had driven off to preside over a magistrates' bench in the local town, Mrs Jenkinson seized the opportunity to totter away to her chamber, adjuring Miss Anne to take her usual afternoon walk in the company of her maid, Polly. Anne, who was intensely bored by Polly's never-ending accounts of beaux in the militia regiment quartered at

Ashford, told the girl that she intended to walk in the shrubbery and so needed no escort.

As soon as Polly was out of sight, Anne made haste to escape through the pleasure gardens and across the bridge that spanned the ha-ha. Then she fled over the meadow and down to the path which followed along the rush-fringed banks of the two artificial lakes. This path was prohibited territory for, although the water was not particularly deep, Anne had never learned to swim. Once or twice, long ago, she had been here in the company of her boy cousins, Darcy and FitzWilliam, but those occasions were half lost in the dreamlike mists of childhood memory. She remembered a waterfall, and a post with a large bird sitting on it, and some thick, dark overhanging yew trees, and a cave or passageway that led through under the waterfall from one side to the other. But were these picturesque and romantic features *really* there, she wondered, or had she invented them; were they products of her youthful imagination?

Anne led such a silent, solitary, unstimulated life that, quite often, she suffered from real uncertainty as to whether an event had taken place, or whether she had dreamed it. Her dreams were more vivid than her waking life. She told herself stories all the time, and these stories had taken over a large part of her mental landscape.

But no! She now discovered there really was a post,

standing out in the middle of the water, with a heron perched on it, just as she had remembered. And now, also, she could hear the rushing sound of the waterfall and see its white gleam. There were the yew trees casting their dark shadows over a high bank ahead, and the brook running down in the little artificial tributary channels spanned by bridges made from single flat rocks. Amazingly, it was all exactly as she recalled. There, too, was the cave entrance, a dark, narrow opening half veiled from view by sheets of falling spray from the cascade.

Anne had not the least intention of venturing anywhere near the cave, let alone going into it, but she was intensely happy to find that it really existed, that it was still there, and not a product of her starved imaginings.

I *shall* go into it sometime, by and by, she thought. With the right companion. When I am grown. I shall go in and walk right through, from one side to the other. Darcy and FitzWilliam did that, I remember. They became very wet, soaked through their jackets and up to their knees, and my Aunt Anne gave them a great scold, and so did Mamma. That was when Aunt Anne was still alive, so it must have been over ten years ago.

Growing accustomed now to the sound of the cascade, Anne began to think that she could hear, as well, a faint sound – a whine, a mew, some plaintive cry – up ahead, at the top of the bank above her.

Retreating back across one of the little rock bridges, she found a path which led on up the bank. Here the stream had been confined to a narrow channel between brick walls, and so induced to pour with considerable force over a stone lip, dropping twelve feet into a pool below, and thus away through the lower pond towards the mill. The water in this sluice ran swift and clear, not more than eighteen inches deep. It was studded, here and there, with large flat rocks, each about the size of a card table, so that a bold and agile person might use them as stepping-stones and pass across to the other side of the stream. For the more timid, the path led on to a conventional wooden bridge, higher up. Anne pursued her course towards the bridge, then came to a stop. For, on one of the rocks in midstream, looking damp and disconsolate and thoroughly out of place, was a large, tawny-yellow cat, which, on seeing Anne as a possible rescuer, opened a vast pink mouth in a frantic, dolorous and peremptory demand for assistance.

Lady Catherine, holding that animals breed dirt and disease, had never allowed pet dogs or cats about Rosings House. But Anne recognized this one, for it belonged to the two painters at Wormwood End cottage who sometimes, in fine weather, took drives about the countryside in an ancient pony-chair, with the cat sitting majestically between them, visibly enjoying the treat quite as well as its two masters.

'You foolish beast!' called Anne. 'How did you ever get yourself there? Come to me, come!'

But the cat, evidently unnerved by the slippery, weed-grown surface of the rock on which it was perched, or the force of the water rushing past it, raised and lowered its front feet in indecision, mewing loudly and piteously.

Anne was not at all courageous and had not the least intention of trying to rescue the cat herself, but her conscience was touched by its plight and she felt that she could not go away and leave it in such a predicament. She made haste to follow the continuation of the path along by the side of the upper lake until she reached the cottage known as Wormwood End. It was an unpretentious little stone-built, slate-roofed dwelling, with a paling fence and an ash path. There was a barn adjoining it, which the two occupiers had turned into a studio.

Receiving no reply to her knock on the cottage door, Anne walked over to the studio and rapped on its door. This was immediately opened by Ambrose Mynges, or 'Young Tom'. He was a Roman-nosed man in his late thirties who looked, from his black curly hair, as if he might have Mediterranean blood. He wore a paint-smeared smock and held a paintbrush in his hand. He appeared surprised and not especially pleased at the sight of his visitor.

'Miss de Bourgh! What brings you here?'

'Oh, sir! Your cat is in trouble, sitting on a rock down where the brook runs so fast. That *is* your cat, is it not? That big yellow one? She is crying most miserably!'

'Our Alice? Yes, indeed! Has the wretch got herself into difficulties again? I am very much obliged to you, Miss de Bourgh – I will come and rescue her directly.'

A voice from the interior now demanded to know what was going on, and Mynges, turning, said:

'Do come in a moment, Miss Anne, while I leave my brush to soak and find a jacket. Tom, here is Miss de Bourgh, arrived to inform us that Alice has got herself marooned on a rock in the rapids.'

He swept a large bundle of blue velvet from a chair and said, 'Pray be seated, Miss de Bourgh. I shall not be more than a couple of minutes.'

Anne moved almost unconsciously to the freed chair and sat down on it. All her intention was focused on the figure who reclined upon a chaise longue at the end of the studio. The figure was merely that of Mr Desmond Finglow, swathed in more of the heavy blue curtain velvet and holding a toasting-fork in his right hand, but he looked so amazingly kingly that she was quite electrified and could only gaze in silent wonder.

Finglow was a man in his seventies with a majestic countenance, a bush of white hair now somewhat retreating from his brow and a wealth of flowing white beard and moustaches. Two luminous blue eyes enhanced his Jove-like appearance.

Smiling, he said, 'I would rise to greet you properly, Miss Anne, but if I did so without Tom's aid I should infallibly trip over all this tangle of canonicals; so I hope that you will excuse me and take the will for the deed. As you may guess, I am representing Neptune for a set of gods and goddesses which have been commissioned from Tom by the Grimsby Press. How very kind of you to come and tell us about our wayward Alice. From time to time she takes these fits of wandering and we are obliged to perform all kinds of heroic and uncongenial antics in order to rescue her. Ah, Tom, sweetheart, will you be so good as to help me out of these draperies before you run off with Miss Anne to rescue the truant?'

'Of course, my dear – there.'

Divested of the blue velvet, wearing a plain white robe and toga, Finglow still made an impressive figure. He said, 'I will exchange these lendings for a more conventional costume while you go with Miss de Bourgh to fetch our wandering puss. Then I think you should offer her a glass of cowslip wine.'

'Alice?'

'No, chucklehead, Miss Anne.'

'Oh, no – I do not think I had better—' Anne began to protest. But Ambrose Mynges, now revealed in conventional breeches and shooting jacket, said, 'Come and show me where she has got to.'

And, of course, when they reached the marooned Alice, perched like Andromeda on her rock, and Ambrose called to her: 'Come along now, you witless creature – I have seen you jump five times that distance!' the cat stretched herself, hunched her shoulders and easily bounded across to the bank, coming to rub herself vigorously against her master's ankles and then stand on her hind legs, sinking her claws into his thigh, until he picked her up, when she sat on his shoulder looking complacent.

'Her ruff is splendid,' said Anne. 'Almost as good as Queen Elizabeth's.'

'And she has a splendid opinion of herself, quite equal to that of the Virgin Queen,' agreed Ambrose. 'It is her constant ambition to catch an eel down there; she has seen them swimming in that race, but I do not think she ever will. Now please come back, Miss Anne, and take a glass of cowslip wine, or a cup of tea if you prefer, in the cottage, and then I will escort you home, for it grows dusky.'

'Oh, I do not think I should—'

But of course Anne allowed herself to be persuaded. They walked back to the cottage, which, in contrast to the wildly untidy studio, was almost spinsterish in its neatness, and the visitor was regaled, most correctly, with tea and macaroons by the hearth. Talk, easy and simple, ran on conventional lines: the weather, birds and flowers to be seen at this time of year, mention of neighbours and happenings in the village. But the glimpse she had been given of the barn – the paints, the pictures in progress and paraphernalia scattered about; above all the free and friendly relations of the two men, even with their cat – gave Anne de Bourgh an intoxicating glimpse of an undreamed-of life, something that lay totally outside any of her previous experience.

From then on, whenever opportunity presented itself, which it did more and more often as Mrs Jenkinson's migraines increased in frequency, and Lady Catherine became more deeply occupied with the commission of peace for the county, and with parish affairs, Anne found chances to slip away for brief, revitalizing visits to Wormwood End cottage. There she learned a little of the history of painting, for the two men had brought a substantial library with them when they quitted London; she learned a little about public affairs, for the friends received a daily paper and discussed it vigorously, often disagreeing; she learned the pleasures of conversation, which was deficient at Rosings, where Lady Catherine expressed her views and the rest of the household remained silent. Best of all, Anne learned that she herself might have some value in the world, for the two Toms, nine times out of ten, seemed genuinely pleased to see her.

'Why, it is Miss Anne! Come in, come in!' If they were tired, out of sorts, or too hard at work, they said so directly, and her feelings were not hurt. Though sometimes, in the latter case, she was allowed in and might sit and observe in silence if she chose. Just occasionally, if Old Tom were at work on a portrait and the sitter was there, Young Tom would warn her, by a gesture at the door, that the time was not propitious. In London, Desmond Finglow had been well known for his fashionable portraits; he had painted Lord D— and the Duchess of N— and even some members of the royal family, and though he said his eyesight was deteriorating, and he found portraits too much of a strain these days, he still occasionally accepted a commission if some neighbour asked for a likeness. Lady Catherine had never made such a request; she was not interested. In the upstairs gallery at Rosings there was a prim portrait of Sir Lewis de Bourgh as a young man by Arthur Davis, looking boyish and bewildered. '*Not* a good likeness,' Lady Catherine said of it dismissively. 'The artist has entirely omitted his strength and manliness.' But she did not care for art of any kind, holding it to be a frivolous waste of time.

Anne once asked Old Tom if he had seen Davis's

portrait of her father, and he told her he had, at the time when it was painted. 'At that period your father and I were good friends, my dear.' But when she asked what he thought of the portrait, he gave voice to rather the same opinion as Lady Catherine. 'Davis did not make much of him. It was a shallow piece of work. There was more to your father than what he saw.'

Eagerly, Anne asked about her father. 'What was he like, Mr Finglow? I was so young when he died.'

'Oh, do call me Tom, my duck; everybody does. What was your father like? He was one of the most lovable characters I have ever met.'

Old Tom sighed. Anne wondered if he thought it a pity that Sir Lewis had married Lady Catherine. But he said only: 'It was a sad waste that he should die at so young an age. He would have settled down and become a fine man – gone into politics, perhaps.'

'Settled down? Was he wild, then?'

'No more than was to be expected of a man his age. But come, Miss Anne; young Tom here is waiting to walk you home.'

There was only one fly in all this delicious ointment.

When Young Tom was escorting Anne back to the ha-ha bridge after her fifth or sixth visit to Wormwood End, they encountered Sydney Smirke, the head gardener at Rosings, who was very slowly and diligently raking the gravel on the far side of the bridge. Smirke greeted Mynges civilly enough, and said, 'I'll see Miss Anne on as far as the shrubbery, sir,' touching his hat. But when Ambrose had gone, Smirke told Anne:

'Lady Catherine come back early and unexpected, Miss Anne, about half an hour past. She was asking where you was got to, and I told her I thought you was in the succession houses with young Joss . . . Least said soonest mended, I thinks.'

Anne was somewhat flustered. 'Oh – oh, thank you, Smirke.'

She had never liked Smirke. He was a dark, slant-eyed man who always seemed in need of a shave, and had a sidelong way of looking and an obsequious way of agreeing with whatever was said to him, at least by his betters.

'I knew her ladyship would not be wishful to hear that you was down so near the water!' Smirke now suggested. 'I knew that.'

He had a smile like that of a crocodile lying in shallow water waiting for its prey.

Anne felt in her pocket. All she had there was half a guinea.

She gave it to Smirke.

'Oh, thank you, Miss Anne! Thank you indeed! I'll tell the boy Joss, shall I, that he's to say you were in the succession houses. If he were to be asked, that is.'

'No,' said Anne more firmly, 'you need not do that. That will not be necessary.'

And she walked on towards the house, trying to make her footsteps sound brisk and decisive.

Since that day she had given Smirke many more half-guineas.

On that first occasion, chancing to encounter the new garden-boy, Joss, as she returned, nervous and pre-occupied, through the kitchen-garden regions on her way to the stable yard and back door, Anne paused a moment and said:

'Were you in the succession houses just now, Joss?'

'Nay, my lady.'

Joss, a tall, open-faced lad with a mop of curly, pale brownish hair, looked startled to death at being asked this question. As well he might; Anne de Bourgh had never addressed him before.

'Did ye want something from there, miss? I could fetch ye aught that ye wanted – a pine, maybe, or a peach?'

'No – no thank you, Joss. How long have you worked here, now?'

''Tis three-quarters of a year, now, miss, come Lady Day.'

'You live in the village?'

'Yes, miss, I lodge with Miss Hurst, that was kin to my ma.'

'Where is your mother, Joss?'

Reared by Lady Catherine, Anne put the question without hesitation, with a straightforward wish to know the answer; it would not have occurred to her that such an enquiry might cause offence.

But Joss, with equal simplicity, replied: 'She be dead, Miss Anne. She died up there in Lunnon town. Dunnamany years 'tis, now. But I wholly craved to come back to Kent, where I was a babby, for I allus remembered the cherries and the primmy-roses on the banks and the king-cupses in Hunsford brook. 'Sides that, I remembered my ma a-saying as how some good luck'd come my way in Kent. What 'twas, she'd not say. But she had Romany blood, my mam did, she was a Smith and come of travellers' kin. She learned me how to read a hand, did Mam; though I haven't the sight, not how she had it. Shall I read your hand for 'ee, Miss Anne?'

'Gracious,' said Anne, rather disconcerted. 'If you like! But I do not believe in such stuff.'

'No more do I – not more 'n half,' said Joss with an ingenuous grin. 'But let's see, then.'

He took Anne's thin white hand in his brown earthy paw and studied the palm. What he saw seemed to surprise him considerably.

'My word, miss. You're a lepper, you are!'

'A leper?' Anne was puzzled. 'Sick? Infectious, you mean?'

'Nay. There be a high hurdle ahead of ye that ye mun lepp over.'

'What *can* you mean?'

But at that moment they were interrupted by Mrs Jenkinson, who came hastening from the back door, exclaiming, 'Miss Anne, Miss Anne! I have been searching for you everywhere! Lady Catherine has been asking for you this half-hour and more!'

III

Letter from Miss Maria Lucas to Mrs Jennings, Berkeley Street, Portman Square, London

My dear madam,

I arrived safe in Kent, thanks to your kind solicitude in having me despatched to my sister's door in your own comfortable carriage. Thanks also to the careful but speedy driving of your excellent coachman, I was delivered at Hunsford parsonage in good time, first, to bid farewell to my brother-in-law Mr Collins (who is now gone into Hertfordshire to wind up the affairs of his deceased cousin, Mr Bennet), and second, to be of some use and company to my sister Charlotte during the period of her confinement. This, I am happy to say, was of comparatively brief duration, without complications, and the outcome being twin boys, bringing the total of her family to four. The new arrivals are strong and thriving, to judge at least by the power of their lungs. In appearance they resemble my brother-in-law, that is, they are plump, red-faced and active.

While still in Hertfordshire I had anticipated that my time during this visit to Hunsford would be entirely passed in quiet, sisterly conversation, embroidering robes for the new arrivals and hemming napkins. But this was not to be. Judge of my delight, dear, *dear* Mrs Jennings, when your most wonderful, most welcome, most undeserved, most unexampled piece of generosity, the Broadwood piano, was delivered to the parsonage door! How shall I ever repay you for this gift! I play on it all day long, for the diversion of my sister, who dearly loves piano music. How very thoughtful of you it was, too, to send such a quantity of sheet music. Our favourite is 'The Battle of Prague' by Kottzwara, but we also love Dibdin's 'Sailor's Adieu', most touching; and the Clementi, and the Niccolò Puccini Overture – indeed, dear madam, we cannot sufficiently thank you, and I shall be happy to play for you, as many hours as you chuse, next time you visit Lucas Lodge, or if I should again spend time beneath your hospitable roof in Berkeley Street on my return from Kent to Hertfordshire.

My sister Charlotte has now quitted her chamber, as she is naturally of an active disposition and never likes to be confined for longer than is absolutely necessary. Charlotte reclines on the sofa knitting, while I play for her diversion. Not for her alone: we do not lack company, since there are several visitors just now up at Rosings House. The first arrivals were a brother and sister, a Mr and Miss Delaval, whose carriage suffered an accident near here in a snowstorm. Miss Delaval sustained an injury to her ankle, and until it is quite mended Lady Catherine has offered them hospitality. My sister Charlotte was not a little astonished at Lady C.'s readiness to entertain these strangers, for she is not used to be so liberal and sociable, except to members of her own family; but the Delavals are such a very agreeable, entertaining pair and make such acceptable inmates at Rosings that, although Miss Priscilla's ankle is now mending, Lady C. hardly knows how to part with them. Mr D., it seems, is knowledgeable regarding horticulture, and spends hours a day, when it is fine, walking about the grounds of Rosings with Lady C., advising her as to an improved arrangement of her parterres and parkland. She listens to him most willingly!

As you may know, the late Sir Lewis de Bourgh demolished the remains of the ancient, picturesque but highly inconvenient Hunsford Castle in order to erect the commodious, modern-planned Rosings House on its site. The house was built in his lifetime, but the gardens, for which he had ambitious plans, were never completed, since his early death put an end to such activities for some years, and Lady Catherine, it seems, took little interest in his projects and has not troubled herself to finish what he began. But Mr Delaval's ideas, apparently, are much to her taste, and meet with her approbation. Meanwhile his sister is attempting to befriend Miss Anne de Bourgh, though in this endeavour, I think, her success is not so marked. Miss D. is herself remarkably elegant, both in wardrobe and deportment, but her attempts to smarten up Miss Anne have so far met with little response. We should soon be able to observe any changes, for they frequently come calling at the parsonage, Miss Delaval propelled in a basket-chair by her brother, as she is not yet equal to a half-mile walk, although I understand she is now able to take short strolls about the pleasure gardens and add her opinion to the discussions. They are so good as to felicitate me on my playing, and often pass pleasant mornings at this house when Lady C. is away from home sitting on her Justices' bench, chatting and listening to all the delightful music you sent.

Did I mention a Colonel FitzWilliam when I was staying with you? He is a son of the Earl of Wrendale, nephew to Lady C., whom I have met here before, on previous visits to Hunsford. He is now engaged to be married to Miss Anne. He arrived here recently, having escorted an elderly brother of Lady C. from his home in Derbyshire. The brother, Lord Luke Sherbrine, has some family business to transact, relating to their sister, the Duchess of Anglesea. We at the parsonage have not been informed as to the details of this, but it seems to give rise to no little anxiety and disagreement. Colonel F. does not come this way very much . . . I expect he will soon return to Derbyshire. He and Miss Anne do not spend much time together, by all accounts. Charlotte says the match has been arranged with a view to fortune, not the affections of the parties concerned, as is customary among that class of person . . .

Miss Anne is having her portrait painted as a wedding gift for her future husband, Colonel Fitzwilliam. This is being kept a secret at present, both from her mother, and from the colonel. I became privy to the secret by chance, for I happened to call on the painter while a sitting was in progress. He lives with a friend, also a painter, in a cottage on the estate here. I had met them on a previous visit, and was returning a book on birds which they had lent to my sister. They are a most engaging pair, not young, most unusually well informed, well bred and conversible. The portrait, painted by the older man, Mr Desmond Finglow, of whom you have probably heard (I believe he is very well known), has caught a quality that is not often seen in Miss Anne – a thoughtful, attentive, eager, listening expression. As I think I may have mentioned before, the poor girl is, in general, decidedly plain, and most of the time wears a dull, downcast look, which intensifies to downright sulks and ill temper at such times as her mother addresses her. This is not greatly to be wondered at, for Lady C.'s remarks to her daughter are mainly severe reprimands or exhortations to sit up and look pleasant. The only time *I* have ever seen her look pleasant was on this occasion, when I chanced upon her in the painters' barn studio, sitting for her likeness. I could hardly have believed it was the same girl! She seemed so happy and at ease, addressing the painters as 'Old Tom' and 'Young Tom' and permitting their cat to sit on her lap. I do wonder, very much, what will happen when the portrait is done and presented and the cat is out of the bag! Old Tom – Mr Finglow – says this will be his last portrait, as his sight is failing, which is very sad. Young Tom, Mr Mynges, tells me that the style of this picture is very different from his former work: the outlines softer and freer, the whole (which he has painted with some difficulty) being intended to convey an image of Miss Anne's interior being rather than her external appearance. I wonder what Lady Catherine will make of it! When I look at the portrait I wish to make friends, achieve a closer acquaintance with Miss Anne. But this she will by no means permit. She is a strange girl. Perhaps she takes after her uncle, Lord Luke, who is decidedly eccentric. But the two seem to get on no better for that . . .

My paper reminds me to conclude now, *dear* Mrs Jennings – also Charlotte's housekeeper, Mrs Denny, is come to tell me that it is the twins' feeding-time, and I am under contract to play the piano during those periods in order to keep them all calm and cheerful.

With very deepest gratitude and love,
Your affectionate friend,

Maria Lucas

'The expression *dusty-foot*,' said Lord Luke, carefully dissecting a pineapple, 'properly derives from *Pié poudré*, a court formerly held at a fair on St Giles's Hill, near Winchester. It was originally authorized by the Bishop of Winton. Similar courts were held elsewhere, at wakes and fairs, for the summary treatment of pedlars and hawkers who had given short measure, to make them fulfil their contracts.'

Lord Luke's sister regarded him with detestation.

'Lucius,' said Lady Catherine, 'will you kindly desist from irrelevant maunderings and tell me what, precisely, it was that Caroline ffynch-Rampling told you in her letter concerning our sister-in-law Adelaide, and her declared intention of altering her testamentary dispositions?'

Lord Luke gazed vacantly at his sister. His pale blue eyes watered a great deal at all times. He now dabbed them with a snowy handkerchief.

He said: 'It is somewhat remarkable that *pige* should be the Norse word for maiden, and *hog* or *og* Gaelic for young persons generally. Thus *ogan* is a young man, and *oige* a young woman. The common notion that "please the pigs" is a corruption of "please the pix" is wholly unworthy of credit.'

'*Luke!* Will you, pray, be so good as to reply to my question?'

'The word *question*, as meaning the application of torture to extract an answer, was used in 1593,' replied her brother. 'Of course it *may* have been employed before that time; how can we tell? But of that date we can be tolerably certain.'

'Lucius. I shall be obliged if you will show me the letter you say you have received from Caroline.'

'Alas, my dear, I fear I must carelessly have left it behind in Derbyshire. Or, perhaps . . . lost it somewhere along the way here. The Derby Stakes, did you know, were instituted by the twelfth earl in 1780, the year after his establishment of the Oaks Stakes. Hence, Derby Day is the second Wednesday of the great Epsom Spring Meeting. Should we, perhaps, make up a party to go there? Do you not think that would make an agreeable outing? My finances are at low ebb, so a lucky bet would recruit them agreeably. I doubt of Epsom's lying much more than fifty miles from Hunsford, hardly more than half a day's journey . . .'

Lady Catherine contained herself with a great effort.

'Lucius! You must be aware of the importance of this matter, or you would not have bestirred yourself to travel all the way from Derbyshire to Kent. You know that our sister-in-law Adelaide inherited a very substantial sum when her father-in-law died?'

'Hmm,' murmured Lord Luke, 'something decidedly havey-cavey there . . .'

'And since both her children perished in the *Arethusa* shipwreck off the Irish coast, there are no direct heirs. It is our plain duty to see that this important property is not assigned away on some foolish, headstrong caprice of Adelaide. You must acknowledge the necessity for firm direction in that quarter?'

'*Quarter*,' vaguely repeated Lord Luke. 'Were you aware that the derivation of that word, as applied to sparing the life of an enemy, comes from an agreement anciently made between the Dutch and Spaniards, that the ransom of a soldier should be one-quarter of his pay? It makes one reflect that the rules of war are no more than some primitive, preposterous game!'

'*Lucius!*'

'My dear Catherine, you know as well as I do that our sister-in-law Adelaide is a law unto herself. Her only response to any suggestion from you, or indeed from myself, would be to act in a manner flat contrary to what was suggested.'

'Yes. And by making use of that propensity she may be guided,' Lady Catherine grimly replied, doing her best to disguise her relief at her brother's sudden descent into rationality.

He sighed and spread out his hands. Lord Luke was a

slight, spare, shrunken man with a few strands of greying hair dispersed tidily and carefully over his balding crown, a receding jaw and two small eyebrows that perched like circumflexes over pale, startled eyes.

'But Catherine,' he said, 'what is your object in all this? *I* have no offspring – thanks to a beneficient Providence which has preserved me from matrimony or any such entanglements – and your daughter Anne is sufficiently provided for. Did you not inform me that she will have a cool fifty thousand to sugar the nuptial pill for poor FitzWilliam? Can it, therefore, really be worth undertaking an embassy to that distasteful island – Great Morran is its name? The trip to Brinmouth itself must occupy several days of fatiguing carriage travel, and that cannot but be followed by a *sea passage*. It does not bear thinking about.'

'If you yourself are so averse to the idea of visiting Adelaide,' retorted his sister, her cheeks flushed with annoyance, 'why, pray, give yourself the trouble of riding all this way into Kent?'

'But my dear Catherine, a visit to Rosings, with its admirable chef, its succession houses, above all its superlative system of heating' – Lord Luke spread out his gnarled hands gratefully to the noble fire – 'must always be a treat, especially at this time of year, when the snow still lies thick upon the Derbyshire hills. (Not that

I do not still regret the picturesque ancestral pile of Hunsford Castle, not that I did not deeply, *deeply* lament its destruction in order to give place to this commonplace example of modern domestic architecture)' – he glanced disparagingly about the large salon – 'but still, if ancestral relics must be rudely done away with it is something if at least they are exchanged for Rumford stoves and a lavish supply of hot water . . . now what, I wonder, might be the derivation of the term succession house? From the succession of crops, do you suppose? Succession *powder*, of course, was the poison employed by the Marquise de Brinvilliers in her poisonings for the benefit of successors – it is said that King James was so murdered by Villiers, Duke of Buckingham . . . Some connection with the succession of crops, I fancy it must undoubtedly be. I will ask that excellent gardener of yours, Smirke – is that not his name? I do trust that he is still in your employ; he has a fine hand with asparagus.

'But to travel to one of the Isles of Scilly, my good Catherine, at this season of spring gales; no, no, my dear sister, you really must hold me excused. *You* are, without a shadow of doubt, the properest person to undertake that mission – that is, if you really consider it worth the trouble and time spent.'

'It is not in the least convenient.' A frown creased Lady Catherine's brow and ran up into her satin turban.

'I have the Dale-Rothburns dining here on Thursday night – I cannot put them off – and Sir Marmaduke and Lady Towers next week.'

'Ah, dear old Marmie, I am always happy to see him again.'

'If you intend to prolong your stay here, Lucius,' said Lady Catherine, 'you *must* tell that man of yours, Sarcot – is that his name? – to be a great deal more civil in his manner to my maid Pronkum.'

'But surely, Catherine,' responded Lord Luke limply, 'surely you will be taking your attendant with you to the isle of Great Morran?'

'Pronkum is quite useless on a ship. She at once becomes completely prostrated by *mal de mer*, and this puts her in such a wicked temper for the week preceding and the week after, that taking her to Great Morran is not to be thought of,' said Lady Catherine irritably. '*If* I go, I must take Hoskins, a woman I have recently hired to assist Pronkum, which is not a satisfactory arrangement. My mind is by no means made up on the matter . . .'

Lord Luke appeared prepared to launch into a series of arguments in favour of his sister's mission, when the Delavals entered the room, Ralph propelling his sister in the basket-chair.

'*So* stupid,' Miss Delaval explained with her quick, mischievous smile. 'I wanted to go as far as the lake – I had heard so much of its beauties – but the walk proved too far for my ankle. Ridiculous me! And the outcome is that I am back on wheels once more. But we interrupt a family conference! Forgive us, we will go into the library.'

'No, no, pray do not think of going, my dear Miss Delaval!' exclaimed Lord Luke. 'You may help to persuade my sister that a visit to the isle of Great Morran at this season of the year can afford her nothing but pleasure – the flowers, the gardens of Morran Manor, I understand, are quite magnificent.'

There had, it seemed, been some slight former acquaintance between Lord Luke and the Delavals; Mardale Place, the crumbling establishment inhabited by Lord Luke in Wensleydale, was not too far distant from Mr Bingley's newly built house, where the brother and sister had recently spent a period of time advising the latter about the layout of his grounds.

'If you are quite sure that we do not intrude . . . My sister and I have been discussing (and admiring) the prospect from your knot-garden, Lady Catherine, and we are entirely agreed upon one point . . .'

Welcoming the change of subject from the Duchess of Anglesea's grounds to her own, Lady Catherine was prepared to listen.

'*All* the views from Rosings are unequalled,' she pronounced. 'But what is it that you have in mind, sir?'

'Oh, madam, you are quite right, they are indeed unequalled, but it seemed to us very unfortunate that from the knot-garden – and, in fact, from the southerly windows on the first and second floors of this house – that scrubby little cottage and shed intrude so wretchedly upon the scene. Without them, or perhaps with some pleasing grotto or classic temple erected to replace them—'

'Humph,' said her ladyship, considering, 'there may be something in what you say.'

She did not observe the appalled expression on the countenance of her daughter Anne.

'Something quite plain – Doric columns, or perhaps a replica of the Parthenon?'

'Is the cottage occupied?' enquired Miss Delaval. 'Will it be necessary to rehouse the occupants if the building is pulled down?'

'The cottage is rented. In such an eventuality the tenants must find themselves other accommodation. That would be their affair. I am under no obligation—'

'But Mamma,' ventured Anne in a very small voice, 'Mr Mynges and Mr Finglow live there. They were Papa's friends.'

'My dear, do not put yourself forward in matters which are no concern of yours,' said Lady Catherine sharply. 'It is most unbecoming.'

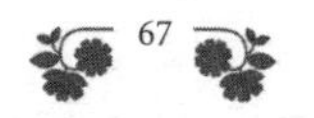

Anne fell silent, Miss Delaval gave her a slight, sympathetic smile, raising her brows as if to say, I perfectly comprehend your feelings, but what can I do?

She has freckles on her nose, thought Anne de Bourgh. Her skin is smooth but thick, like the pith of an orange. It is not so fine as my skin, or that of Maria Lucas, who has a very delicate, clear complexion, though somewhat pale. I do not trust Miss Delaval. She reminds me of the cat Alice . . .

IV

At this season Anne de Bourgh frequently rose before six, comfortably conscious that nobody else in the mansion who might be likely to pursue her with reprimands and prohibitions would be stirring for some time yet.

Her first objective was a cherry orchard, which lay to the east of the vegetable gardens. In early morning the rays of the sun rising over Hunsford Hill caught the white blossom here and turned it to a spectacular dazzle.

'Merrily, merrily, shall I live now, Under the blossom that hangs on the bough,' Anne murmured to herself, staring up at the snowy canopy. 'Oh, *how* I should like to have a cherry orchard of my very own.'

'But all this'll be yourn one day, will'n it, missie?' said Joss the garden-boy, coming up beside her with a trug full of turnips, his black-and-white mongrel dog Pluto following behind.

'Yes,' sighed Anne, 'but by then I shall be married to my cousin FitzWilliam. And I heard him yesterday agreeing with the Delavals that this orchard should be cut down because the trees are old, too big; picking the fruit takes too much labour, and in any case the orchard cuts off the view of the lake from the library windows. I do not imagine that I will have any say in the matter.'

'That do seem wholly unfair,' remarked Joss, 'when 'tis through you that the orchard come to be his'n. But there! Things hardly ever is fair.' He whistled a few bars of 'Cherry Ripe', and added inconsequentially, 'My mam used to make wondrous good dried cherries. 'Twas a receipt she told me she had from Mrs Godwin the parson's lady.'

'The one before Mrs Collins,' said Anne. 'She died when I was a baby. I never tasted her dried cherries. I'll ask Mrs Collins if she still has the receipt; I believe that when the Collinses moved into the parsonage, they found a number of old books that had belonged to the Godwins. There may be a receipt book among them.'

'I'd best get on,' Joss remarked, 'or Cook'll have my tripes for pot-holders.' Noticing Anne's downcast expression, he added, 'Come, you, missie, and see my Pluto take his morning dip. That always rouse your sperrits.'

Between the cherry orchard and the knot-garden lay a small walled courtyard enclosing a fountain. This consisted of a bowl, raised on a pedestal about four feet above the flagged pavement, with a series of smaller basins above, each less in circumference than the one below, topped by a spout of water thrown upwards to fall back from basin to basin. The bottom one, somewhat larger than a hip bath, was greatly favoured by Pluto, who now sprang up into it, rolled himself luxuriously under the sheets of water that fell from above, then jumped down to the ground and shook himself with vigour. Anne laughed, as she always did, at this enjoyable scene, while keeping herself safely distant from the flying drops of spray.

'Again, Joss! Make him do it again!'

Joss whistled between his teeth, but Pluto needed no urging and repeated the procedure with enthusiasm.

'Come on now, boy, or us'll be in trouble,' said Joss, and strode off whistling.

Ralph Delaval, returning from an early-morning excursion to the village of Hunsford, thought what a startling improvement laughter made to Anne de Bourgh's looks.

'Good morning!' he greeted her. 'Have you, like myself, been calculating what a fine crop of cherries there will be? We must persuade Lady de Bourgh to postpone the execution of the orchard until the crop has been gathered in.' He noticed how her expression at once fell back into its habitual look of sour withdrawal.

'It is no use wasting your civilities on Anne de Bourgh,' his sister Priscilla had said to him. 'She is betrothed to her cousin and resigned to it.'

'You could put out your best arts and entice him from her,' suggested Ralph.

'He has no money.' Priscilla's tone was sad but resigned. 'If I were ten years younger I could break my heart over him as I see Maria Lucas doing, but unless some windfall comes his way – that aunt in the Scillies – no, no, I am past the age for such follies. I *think*! Now: if Anne were to die, after he married her; if he were to become a wealthy widower—'

'Come, come, my love!' her brother said, laughing. 'Enough of such morbid imaginings! We must address ourselves to the task in hand . . .'

'I know, I know! We might do better in London. If you, dear brother, had not lost such a large sum at Garthover Chase—'

'It was unfortunate,' he said, shrugging. 'How was I to know that Carrick would be there also? I had to give him his revenge.'

'I am so glad that I am not a man, subject to such a ridiculous code of honour. And how fortunate it is that neither Lord Luke nor FitzWilliam are card-minded.'

'Fortunate indeed, since neither can afford to lose. But a few games of whist would pass the time until madam comes to a decision.'

'You are certain that she will do so?'

'Oh, yes,' he said with casual confidence.

Now, looking at Anne de Bourgh with the same instant judgement, he saw there was no possibility of cajoling or ingratiating himself into her favour; so he bowed, raised his hat and made for the glasshouses, where he would be fairly sure of encountering Smirke.

Anne walked in the other direction, towards the lake.

Down at the parsonage, Maria had been providing her usual musical accompaniment for the breakfast of her twin nephews.

'How quiet the house seems when they are both asleep,' she remarked at the end of this ceremony when the infants, replete, were fathoms deep in slumber, each in his own osier basket.

'I miss Sam and Lucy,' Charlotte said. 'I think I shall send for them tomorrow. The house is too quiet without children's voices. It must have been sad indeed in the time of the Godwins.'

'Had they no children?'

'No, she died in childbirth, poor thing. And the child

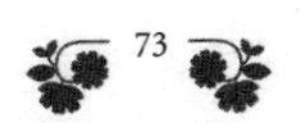

died too, I believe, not immediately but later, during the typhus epidemic. So Mr Godwin became a disconsolate widower and was happy to move to Canterbury when he was offered a stall. Lady Catherine and he, you know, did not always see eye to eye; he did not take such pains, as Mr Collins does, to see matters from her point of view at all times.'

'And his wife, Mrs Godwin? What sort of person was she?'

'Much younger than her husband. Very young and pretty. So I hear from Mrs Hurst, and people in the village. She was a great walker, and knew a deal about birds and flowers and where rare orchids were to be found. Lady Catherine, I believe, did not wholly approve of her, and said that it was a judgement on her, for all her gadding about the woods and meadows, that she died in childbed. But she was quite a favourite with Sir Lewis, I understand; he too was interested in hellebores and monkey orchids, which it seems are to be found in abundance in these parts. Among the Godwins' books I found a little manual of orchids that he had given her.'

'Perhaps they went botanizing together.'

'Oh, I do not think Lady Catherine would have approved of that.'

'I wonder if he can have been a sensible man? I

cannot imagine that a sensible man would have married Lady Catherine.'

'She may have been different when she was younger,' Charlotte said hesitantly. 'Perhaps their families obliged them to marry, like—' She stopped.

'And he was *very* rich – and handsome too,' Maria went on. 'Where did his money come from?'

'From the manufacture of some garment, I believe.'

'So she determined to snabble him. And then she could pull down the ruins of Hunsford Castle and build herself a fine modern mansion.'

'While he consoled himself with orchids and the vicar's lady.'

'We should not say such things, even in jest.'

The doorbell rang, and after a moment or two Mrs Denny came in with a note for Mrs Collins.

'It is from Lady Catherine,' Charlotte said, reading it. 'She asks if I can spare you for the evening, tonight, when she is expecting the Dale-Rothburns to dinner, and Sir Marmaduke Towers with his lady.'

'I am to *dine* with them?' Maria was hardly less appalled than startled.

'Oh *no*, my dear! I am surprised that you should even think of such a thing. No, no, you are to go in afterwards, when they are taking tea, to play and sing for them.'

'Oh, how terrible!' Maria turned pale. 'Charlotte, must I?'

'I think you must, love. Lady Catherine would be very displeased if you declined – and I do not like to think how upset Mr Collins would be.'

'But Colonel FitzWilliam will be there – and the Delavals. I shall feel like a juggler; like some sort of paid entertainer!'

'Except that you will not be paid,' said Charlotte drily.

'It is so demeaning!'

'You have played many times for our father's club, at Lucas Lodge.'

'Yes, but that was for Papa – quite different.'

'I am very sorry for you. But you are well endowed with spirit and dignity. Your courage will carry you through, when it comes to the point.'

'Now you are trying to talk me round, Charlotte. Oh, very well! You may write Lady Catherine my polite acceptance. I shall be most happy. That will not be the truth. I shall hate it and be miserable, every minute that I am there. How can I play the songs that I used to sing for *him*, last summer? Oh, Charlotte, it must mean *something* when two people have so many ideas, so many tastes and feelings in common, must it not?'

'You still love him,' said Charlotte sadly.

'Oh, Charlotte, I do, I do.'

'Well, you must battle against it!' scolded Charlotte. 'That is all we *can* do, you know. And we women are lucky in that respect, unbelievably lucky, that we do have so many useful and agreeable tasks in the performance of which we can divert our minds from such fruitless pains as beset us. Employ yourself. Do you want to go into the kitchen and help Bessie with the bread? You make better bread than she does. Or will you weed my rose-bed, where, Smarden tells me, the celandine is already beginning to show? Or will you walk to the village and execute some commissions for me there, and call in at Mrs Hurst's cottage in Dumb Woman's Lane, to tell her that Sam and Lucy may come home tomorrow, and she is to have their clothes ready washed?'

'I will do that,' said Maria. 'And I will take Sam and Lucy for a walk down Dumb Woman's Lane to look for primroses.'

'Very well. Sam and Lucy will be overjoyed to see you. But' – Charlotte directed a keen glance at her sister – 'you are not going to the village in the hope of encountering Colonel FitzWilliam, are you?'

'No, Charlotte. *Truly*.'

'Very well. While you get your hat and pelisse, I will be making out a list.'

Hunsford village consisted of a few brick and tile-hung

cottages assembled round a green, an oast house and the Hopsack Inn, a tolerably commodious establishment, thatched and weatherboarded. Once it had been somewhat marred by ill fame, spoken of as a resort of smugglers. But those days were long gone by. In the centre of the green was a quintain, a tilting-post, mistakenly assumed by strangers to be a flagpole adorned with some odd appendages; this, too, would long since have been consigned to the dust-heap of history, but Sir Lewis de Bourgh had been proud of it and had added a clause to his will providing for its annual repainting and refurbishment.

Maria Lucas had spoken truly to her sister when she asserted that she did not go to the village in hope of encountering Colonel FitzWilliam there; she was therefore not a little dismayed on reaching the green to recognize his tall, unmistakable figure across the grass, outside the post office, beside Miss Delaval in her basket-chair. A moment later Mr Delaval joined them, emerging from the post office.

The very last thing Maria felt inclined for, just then, was light-hearted conversation with the Delavals in company with the colonel; she had not greatly taken to the brother and sister, and wished they would put an end to their visit and quit Rosings. But Miss Delaval's ankle seemed to provide them with sufficient reason for indefinitely prolonging their stay.

Before they could recognize and greet her, Maria turned down Dumb Woman's Lane, a small byway leading to the mill, and knocked at the door of Mrs Hurst's cottage. The door was opened by Mrs Hurst's widowed sister, Mrs Hobden, who shared the cottage with her, and at present played the principal part in the care of the parsonage children.

'Oh, come in, miss, come in, do! Mester Sam and Miss Lucy'll be main pleased to see ye! They'm out at the back – young Joss fettled them up a see-saw. He be out there with them now; 'tis his breakfast hour. Come through the house, won't 'ee; I'm this minute a-washing their shifts and shirts, ye won't mind the steam.'

The house consisted of one room and a back kitchen, and a ladder leading to the upper floor. From visits to cottages at Longbourn, Maria was instantly familiar with the sour smell of damp brick floor, damp, much-used rags, potatoes boiled in their skins, damp lath-and-plaster walls and stuffiness from windows that were never opened. She passed through the lean-to back kitchen, which held little more than a copper basin of laundry perched in a brick housing and heated over a fire of twigs and rubbish. Mrs Hobden gave the steaming wash a stir with a stick as she passed by, then called out of the back door:

'Miss Lucy! Mester Sam! Here's your auntie come a-visiting!'

The joyful shrieks outside grew louder. Maria stepped out into the small, hedged-in space enclosing a patch of worn grass, a vegetable bed with two rows of cabbages and a muddy hen-run where a flock of brown poultry pecked at cabbage stalks. On the grass a see-saw had been constructed by the simple process of laying a plank over a massive section of tree trunk turned on its side; tumbling off this, muddy and joyful, were Charlotte's two elder children. With them was a tall, brown-faced boy whom Maria recalled seeing sometimes at work, in the grounds of Rosings House. He was, she knew, a nephew or cousin of Mrs Hurst, and lodged with her.

He touched his forelock and gave Maria a friendly grin.

'I've come to take them for a walk,' she said, 'but perhaps they'd rather stay and play on the see-saw with you.'

'Nay, miss, I'm bound to get back to work. I'll walk with ye part of the way, then take the kitty-corner cut over the meadow.'

They set off down the lane, the children swinging on Joss's arms till he begged for mercy.

'How will I ever do my digging if ye pull my arms out o' their sockets?'

As they walked, they talked about the shocking forthcoming improvements at Rosings.

'By my way of thinking, 'tis a shame to cut down the cherry orchard,' Joss said. 'That 'ud furnish a-plenty cherries for years yet.'

'It does seem a pity,' agreed Maria.

'And as for putting those two poor gentlemen out o' their home – that's downright *wicked*! (Ye won't mind what I say, missie, ye won't tell Lady Catherine?)'

'Which two poor gentlemen?' said Maria, startled. 'I don't know what you mean?'

'Hadn't ye heard, then? 'Tis Owd Tom and Young Tom – Mester Finglow and Mester Mynges, the painting gentlemen. They've been handed notice to quit after thirty-odd years!'

'Oh, good gracious,' said Maria. 'That's terribly sad. But why?'

'So Lady Catherine can put up a gazey-boo there, so 'tis said. A Grecian temple. They say poor Mester Finglow – Owd Tom, as we call him – was so palsy-strook when he heard that, he fell down in a swound. He's mortal ill, you know, missie, he bain't long for this world.'

'No, I didn't know,' said Maria. 'That is really dreadful. But perhaps when Lady Catherine hears how ill he is, she will change her mind.'

'Perhaps,' said Joss. 'Perhaps carrots will grow on tree-tops.'

He swung over a stile, waved to the children and set off across the fields.

'Come, children,' said Maria. 'Let's go and look for primroses.'

She took their hands and set off down the lane with a heavy heart.

Before reaching the mill, the lane passed through a patch of hazel known locally as the Dilly Woods, because of the wild daffodils that grew there. A small brook, babbling between low ferny banks, made its way through this wood and down to the mill, passing under an arched stone bridge where it met the track. Here the children were happy to spend many minutes dropping twigs into the water on one side, and then hastening to make sure that they emerged on the other. Maria, sitting on the parapet, watched them and thought her own troubled thoughts.

Presently she was roused by the sound of footsteps and saw the figure of a man approaching through the trees. FitzWilliam! was her first startled reaction, and then she excoriated herself for her stupidity; had she not seen him in the village, going precisely in the opposite direction? Besides, this was a shorter, slighter man of wholly different build, nothing like the colonel. As he drew closer she saw that it was Ambrose Mynges, whom she had met with Charlotte when returning a borrowed book to the two painters.

He looked sad and harassed, and she did not wonder, remembering what the boy Joss had told her.

She bade him good morning, trying to put all she could of friendly sympathy into her voice.

'Mr Mynges! Good day to you.' She saw that he hardly recollected her, and added, 'I am Mrs Collins's sister from the parsonage, taking my niece and nephew for an outing.'

'Oh, yes. Miss – Miss Lucas, is it not? I am, that is, I am on my way, but perhaps – I wonder if you can possibly help me?'

'Of course! If I can. What may I do for you? How can I be of assistance?'

'My friend Desmond is very ill. Mr Willis the surgeon is with him now. His condition is acutely serious: cordials, compresses, bleeding, clysters, cupping – no efforts have been spared, but none has been of any use. Mr Willis is of the opinion that only skilled nursing can save him now. There is a Mrs Hobden, who, according to Willis, might be the very person, if she is available.'

'Oh, yes, I know Mrs Hobden,' said Maria at once. 'We all know Mrs Hobden, do we not, children? She has been looking after this pair. But I will take them home directly and ask her to come to you. I am sure she will be glad to do so. Pray do not trouble yourself any further. Mr Mynges; go back to your friend. I will deliver your message to Mrs Hobden, and I am sure she will be on her way to you within the hour.'

'Can you really do so?' His gaze had been directed at the ground, frowning, preoccupied; but now he looked straight at her, and she saw how full of suffering were his dark eyes.

'Yes, sir! I promise faithfully. And if Mrs Hobden, for some reason, is unable to come, I will see that she finds somebody else, of equal skill. Go back to your friend,' Maria repeated. She added, 'I heard – I have been told of what happened – of the bad news that caused your friend's collapse, and I was more shocked than I can say, shocked and sorry. But I will keep you no longer. Good day! Come children, we must hurry back to Mrs Hobden.'

'But we haven't picked any primmy-roses,' objected Sam.

'No; we are going to do something even nicer than that; we are going to collect your toys in a basket from Mrs Hobden, and then I am going to take you home to Mamma. How about that?'

'Oh, *yes*! Home to Mamma!' Both children began to dance and caper.

Involuntarily Maria smiled over their heads at Mr

Mynges, but he had already turned and was hastening back down the path along which he had come.

Poor man, thought Maria, walking back with the children along Dumb Woman's Lane. His troubles are far worse than mine.

On their way back to Rosings House Colonel FitzWilliam and the Delavals encountered Lord Luke Sherbrine, taking a gentle stroll along the gravelled driveway.

'Ah, my dear Fitz! So there you are! I was wanting the favour of a quiet word with you. Felt a touch of my old trouble coming on, thought it best to get matters settled before, in case I was obliged to retire to my bed – devilish inconvenient that would be – not knowing your plans, when you wish to return to Derbyshire – hey?'

'Oh, my plans are unfixed at present, sir,' replied the colonel. 'I am entirely at your disposal.'

'Lucky Lord Luke!' remarked Miss Delaval, with her elfin grin.

'Ah – just so!' Lord Luke's pale eyes surveyed the lady, then rested on the colonel.

'I will take my sister into the house,' said Delaval, and to his sister: 'You must repose and refresh yourself for the evening, you know, my dear, when you will be expected to shine amid the company.'

'Oh, yes! And we are to hear the gifted and delightful

Miss Lucas play and sing.' Miss Delaval glanced at the colonel, who reddened and looked away. She added pensively, 'What a pity I did not bring my harp with me on this excursion. Then I could have lent my assistance to Miss Lucas.'

'You forget, my love,' her brother pointed out, 'you would not have been able to play the harp. Your ankle . . .'

'Yes, yes, of course, my ankle. What a poor honey I am. Take me into the house, Ralph.'

The lady was wheeled away.

'Humph! What d'you make of them, really – hey, Fitz?' enquired Lord Luke, when the Delavals were a safe distance away.

'A charming pair, do you not think so, sir?'

'Charming riff-raff! I'd give a monkey to know what they are saying to each other at this moment. Would not you, Fitz? You had best watch out for yourself, my boy; one word over the line from you and she'd have you in the matrimonial noose. I know that breed – mark me!'

'Oh, no, sir, you are quite out there. I'll lay she knows my rent roll to the last sixpence. She is after bigger game. But what did you wish to say, sir?'

'When my sister has left for Morran . . .'

'You are quite certain that she will go, sir?'

'Oh, yes, my boy. She don't show it, but she is in a regular ferment over the thought that Adelaide might leave her fortune away from the family. She won't rest till she has done her possible best to see that money safely bestowed on somebody of her own recommendation – on Anne if she can.' FitzWilliam sighed. 'Why sigh, my boy? Then the cash would end up in your pocket, you'd be a man of means – no bad thing, hey? But that ain't to the purpose. What I want is to have at least three weeks here at Rosings before Catherine returns.'

'*Why*, sir?'

'That's my business, my boy. But I'll let you into my confidence so far as to tell you that I was *devilish* displeased when Catherine – without a by your leave from the family – pulled down Hunsford Castle and clapped that flat-fronted monstrosity in its place! Crumbling the castle may have been, draughty it certainly was, but it had dignity, it had quality, it had antiquity and tradition, whereas that object – pah! I'd as soon look at my snuff-box – sooner!'

'Why didn't you protest when it was done, sir? You were a friend of Sir Lewis – why didn't you say something to him? Or to my father?'

'Pooh – your father: he has no time for affairs here. Up to his ears in politics. Besides, I was in India at the time. I had enough to do, earning my living. When I got back to England, the thing had happened. There were not two stones of the castle still standing. And, what's more, I had property, belongings in Hunsford Castle – dammit, Fitz, it was the family home where I grew up. Half my life had been spent there. Now where is all that stuff, where are all those things?'

'Well,' said FitzWilliam, 'where are they?'

'Do you think I didn't ask Catherine that question? Oh, she says vaguely, a lot of old rubbish was thrown away. Some things were put up in the attics. Yes, there are attics at Rosings House, it seems. May I look in the attics? No, certainly not! Look in the attics, what next? What would the servants say, to have you rummaging about up there? What do I care what the servants say? I want time to go through those attics, box by box, parcel by parcel. And Catherine will never permit that. But when she's off in Great Morran, arguing with Adelaide – d'ye see? Hey?'

'Yes, sir, I think I begin to see.'

V

Letter from Maria Lucas to Mrs Jennings

My dear madam,

The spring in Kent is very beautiful. I can well understand why this county is called the Garden of England. The trees are covered in young leaves and white blossom, the woods and lane banks are carpeted in white violets and anemones. Longbourn in Hertfordshire cannot compare, and though I am sometimes homesick I am happy to be here with Charlotte, who has always been my favourite sister. Mr Collins is still absent, for his legal business at Longbourn Manor is not yet completed. Lady Catherine is very indignant about this, and roundly scolds poor Charlotte, but Mr Delaval remains at Rosings, and conducts the Sunday services with the curate, Mr Lawson, so she has no real grounds for complaint, especially as

Mr Delaval has become a great favourite with her. (I do not myself greatly care for Mr Delaval.) In any case, Lady Catherine herself sets off, three or four days from now, to pay a visit to her sister-in-law, the Duchess of Anglesea. (The Duke is not there; he is off commanding various regiments in Spain.) Mr Gregory Stillbrass, Lady C.'s attorney from Canterbury, has been here so that she could grant him a power of attorney while she was away from home. (I believe her brother Lord Luke, also visiting Rosings, was very offended that the power was not signed to him, but Lady Catherine has no great opinion of his capacities.) They are a strange family, indeed. I was able to observe them the other evening when I was summoned to play and sing for guests who were invited to dinner. (I wore the pale rust-pink muslin that you were so kind as to give me, dear Mrs Jennings.) I sat in the music room, which adjoins the great blue-and-gold salon, and the double doors were open wide, so I was able to see and hear much that went on. Col. FitzWilliam was sometimes so kind as to turn the pages for me, but in general I might have been a block of wood, for all the notice that was paid.

Lady Catherine was amazingly grand, in crocus-coloured satin and a headdress at least two feet in height, adorned with ostrich feathers. But what made her costume outstanding was the profusion of diamonds that she had hung about her person: a triple-strand necklace, ear-bobs, innumerable brooches and a kind of coronet wound about her turban.

Many were the compliments she received upon her garniture, but I happened to hear Miss Delaval remark privily to Lady Towers that since the diamonds were so fine, it was a great shame that they had been allowed to grow so dirty. Lady C. also chanced to overhear this, and was mightily displeased, and I noticed her several times afterwards observing herself narrowly, in one of the long glasses which alternate with the blue-and-gold panelling. Next, she asked Sir Marmaduke Towers if he could recommend a good diamond-cleaning establishment and he, without the least hesitation, suggested Gray's, at 41 Sackville Street, but now Mr Delaval, approaching, contradicted him and said no, Rundell & Bridge were more reliable, and, furthermore, would send a man to the country who would perform the task of cleaning the diamonds on the premises, thus avoiding the expense and risk of transporting the stones to London. Lady C. took heed of all this, but what decision she came to regarding the jewellery I do not know.

Miss Anne de Bourgh was greatly out of spirits throughout the whole evening, and more than once I heard her being reprimanded by her mother for her downcast looks and mumchance manner. 'How can you expect me to be otherwise,' said Miss Anne, 'when poor Mr Finglow lies so ill, and it is all because of what you did.' 'How dare you speak to your parent in such a manner,' replied Lady C. in a passion. 'Let me hear no more of this!' 'If my father were still alive—' said Miss Anne, but Lady C., with a terrible look, said, 'Hold your tongue, miss!' and swept away.

The cause of this dissension is that the two painting gentlemen (I mentioned them in a previous letter) who live in a cottage by the lake have been given notice to quit, so that their house may be pulled down and some elegant folly or grotto erected in place of it, which will more suitably enhance the distant prospect from Rosings House. They had occupied their cottage for such a long time that this was a severe blow to them, and the elder of the two men, Mr Desmond Finglow, already in poor health, suffered at that time from a palsy-stroke which has left him blind and helpless. It is very sad to see him. Charlotte and I have been several times to the house with fruits and jellies, but Mr Willis the surgeon holds out no real hope that the gentleman will recover. A further pity is that the portrait which Mr Finglow was painting of Miss Anne was so nearly finished, but he can no longer see it, nor would have the strength to complete it. Meanwhile his friend Mr Ambrose has been looking about for another house to which they might remove, but this is no easy task, as you may imagine, and he has little heart for it, with his friend so ill. I believe he appealed to Lord Luke and asked him if Lady C. might not be prepared to revoke her edict, but Lord L. is a queer, unaccountable character. He seems amiable enough, but will not bestir himself for any other person. And he said (probably with truth) that he has no influence with his sister – as indeed who has, unless the advice chimes with her own wishes? Her answer was merely that when she returns from the island of Great Morran she hopes to find the cottage vacated and the process of demolition begun.

Meanwhile, turning to a more cheerful topic, my niece and nephew, little Lucy and Sam, have returned home as their foster mother, Mrs Hobden, has gone to nurse poor Mr Finglow. They are a dear pair of children, and you will be happy to hear that I am teaching them to play on your beautiful piano, which they take to most readily, and they are also happy to caper about for ever while I play them country dances. The twin babes thrive and my sister Charlotte is quite restored to her normal busy self. I should be thinking of my return into Hertfordshire, but Charlotte begs me to continue here so long as Mr Collins is from home, and indeed I am happy to do so.

I have been trying to befriend poor Miss Anne, who, I think, has a sad life of it, and sees little good ahead in her future, but she responds only very slowly to my overtures. Her chief friend seems to be Joss, the garden-boy, who was brought up in London by a gypsy mother but returned to Hunsford, his birthplace, after her death. He seems to have had a most varied life: at one time he worked for Sir Felix Ravenstone, the President of the Royal Society; at another, he told me, he trained as a pickpocket! And his dog, Pluto, was also trained to the trade! I hope he was funning. He is an entertaining boy, with a quiet wit. At all events, there are few pockets to pick in rural Kent.

Your sincere friend,

Maria Lucas

'The earliest hangman whose name survives was called Bull. Is not that interesting?' said Lord Luke. 'One asks oneself if it is because of him that the English have adopted John Bull as their national figure. The most famous hangman, of course, was Jack Ketch, who executed Lord Russell and the Duke of Monmouth.'

'Will you please quit this disagreeable topic, Lucius,' snapped Lady Catherine. 'Heaven knows that I have enough to concern my mind without your—'

'A hangman's wage,' her brother pursued, wholly ignoring Lady Catherine's interruption, 'was thirteen pence and a halfpenny – with another three halfpence for the rope. I dare say it is considerably more nowadays. Nobles, of course, were expected to remunerate the executioner with seven or ten pounds for cutting off their heads. That, to me, seems unfair. Why should I be expected to lay out such a sum for such a dismal service?'

'I dare say you would be glad enough to do so when it came to the point, Uncle Luke,' said Anne de Bourgh, rousing herself from a gloomy abstraction. 'Hanging seems to be such a chancy process.'

'Anne! Pray be silent if you have nothing better to say!'

Mr Delaval came hastily to the rescue of this unfortunate conversation.

'Shall I write to Rundell and Bridge, Lady Catherine, and invite them to send their diamond expert down so that he may be burnishing up your necklace while you are on your travels? Then what a joy when you come back, to see you and the stones complementing each other in perfection! I trust you will give a party for the whole neighbourhood after your safe return?'

'Yes indeed,' chimed in his sister. 'And my brother will have all manner of happy surprises prepared for you then. But mum is the word! I must not reveal his secrets until that joyful day!'

'Humph,' said her ladyship. 'I have not yet made up my mind about the necklace. Sir Marmaduke recommended Gray's of Sackville Street – he said they did an excellent piece of work for him on the hilt of the sword that Charles the First gave his ancestor. Myself, I incline to Gray's. Pronkum could take the jewels up to London.'

'Pronkum!' cried Sir Luke in outrage. 'You would entrust your diamonds to that skinny creature?'

'She has served me faithfully for twenty years. I place my complete trust in her.'

'I'd put more trust in a scarecrow. And a scarecrow would be better company.'

'Mr Ambrose Mynges is here, my lady,' said Frinton the butler, entering, 'and begs the honour of a few words with you.'

'I cannot see him at this present,' said Lady Catherine shortly. 'Tell him that I am too occupied. I have a great many affairs to attend to. Lucius, why do not you see him? Frinton, tell the man that Lord Luke will see him.'

'What good will *that* do, Catherine?' said Lord Luke fretfully. But Lady Catherine had already left the breakfast parlour.

Anne went out and walked unhappily towards the pleasure gardens. She could not bear the thought of her friends being rebuffed.

A stretch of lawn, dotted with a few trees, lay between the rear of the house and the pleasure gardens. Here the boy Joss was to be seen, equipped with a broom and a shovel, carefully inspecting the verdure. His dog Pluto followed him as usual.

'What in the world are you doing, Joss?' Anne asked, as she came up with him. 'It is not the season for dead leaves. Or mushrooms.'

'No, missie,' said Joss with a broad grin. ''Tis badger fewmets I be looking for.'

'*Badger fewmets?* What are they?'

'Droppings, miss. Turds. Owd Mester Brock, he be a-coming this way, of a night, every night just now, and doing his business out on the grassy lawn. Like, maybe, 'tis to claim the ground as hisn, warn off other badgers.' His eye spotted a pile of the material in question, and he neatly swept it on to the shovel with the broom and then dropped it into a bucket.

'What do you *do* with them?'

'Put them on the rose-bed, missie. Powerful good for the roses, they do be.'

'How do you know it is a badger and not just a dog?' Anne said, looking sceptically at Pluto. 'The droppings look much the same size to me.'

'Oh, no, missie. Badgers' fewmets be full o' nuts and berries – holly berries, yew berries, rose-hips – a dog, he won't ever nibble such stuff, will 'ee, Pluto?'

Pluto looked up and wagged his tail.

'But 'tis a right nuisance, that it be,' Joss acknowledged, 'and the sooner Mester Brock finds hisself another privy for to leave his leavings in, the better I'll be pleased. Mester Smirke, he's worried her ladyship'll walk this way some morning afore I've tidied up, and then the fur'd fly, surely!'

'It certainly would!'

Sighing, Anne walked on past the shrubbery, and came to the bridge over the ha-ha. From here there was a clear view down to the house that her friends had soon to quit. She stood wretchedly on the bridge, wishing that she would go down and comfort them, aware that she could do nothing, enraged at her own helplessness.

A thick column of smoke rose from beside the cottage. Sometimes a leaping flame could be seen.

Smirke walked past Anne, wheeling a barrow full of hedge clippings. He greeted Anne very respectfully, then, following the direction of her gaze, said with a knowing grin:

''Tis like the gentry down there be a-clearing up and a-tidying out. Her ladyship 'on't want any of their clutter left behind when they do go.'

'But how *can* they go when poor Mr Finglow is so unwell?' she said angrily.

'That be their affair, bean't it?'

He wheeled his load away to where a bonfire of his own, beside the glasshouses, piled high with greenstuff, was sending a thick, lazy plume of grey smoke into the still air.

Lady Catherine could be seen emerging from the house, accompanied by the Delavals. Anne hastily turned and fled off into the shrubbery.

* * *

The day of Lady Catherine's departure for the island of Great Morran was wet and thundery, a circumstance that effectually prevented any prolonged ceremony of leave-taking. There were two coaches, a baggage coach and the lady's own chaise, in which she rode, escorted by Hoskins, the deputy lady's maid, with a hot brick for her feet wrapped in sheepskin, flasks of hot soup wrapped in felt containers, a cloak bag, umbrellas, a basket of provisions, several volumes of sermons, smelling salts and pills for seasickness.

The horses stood stamping and steaming in the downpour.

Lady Catherine herself was imposingly attired in a plum-coloured pelisse buttoned up to the throat, a huge sable muff and a long sable cloak around her shoulders. Her hat was adorned with egret feathers so long and flexible that they swept the ceiling of the carriage.

Hoskins threw a triumphant glance at the rejected Pronkum, who stood glaring balefully on the steps. There, too, among a group of people getting wet, was Mr Gregory Stillbrass the lawyer, a thin, worried, grey-headed man who did not at all approve of his employer's departure over land and sea on such a hazardous mission.

'But this course is incumbent upon me, do you not

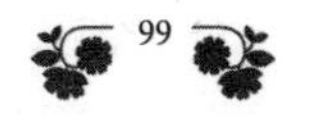

see,' Lady Catherine repeated for the last time as she left him. 'I should never forgive myself if, for lack of effort on my part, such a sum of money were allowed to pass out of the family.'

'But could not Lord Luke, or even I myself—?' He wrung his hands.

'Fiddlesticks, man! Neither of you would be the slightest use. But I am not nobody, I believe.'

'No, *indeed*, your lady is not nobody—'

'And I hope I shall be able to prevail upon my sister-in-law to dispose of that fortune in a rational manner. Where is Anne?' said her ladyship, looking round.

Mrs Jenkinson fluttered forward.

'I am afraid poor Miss Anne is still wholly prostrated—'

'Oh humph. All I can say is that it was all most unfortunate. Most . . .'

'Your ladyship,' called the coachman, 'we should be on our way or we shall never reach Salisbury by dinnertime.'

'Oh, very well. Very well.'

She climbed into the carriage with the assistance of FitzWilliam, and said to him, 'I look to you and Delaval, both men of some sense, to have an eye to all matters about the house while I am gone. My brother is quite useless. And Anne will not come out of her sulks, I suppose, for some considerable time. Mrs Collins! Pray inform your husband that if he is not back at Hunsford before my return, I shall be most seriously displeased.'

'Yes, your ladyship.'

'Yes, Aunt Catherine,' Colonel FitzWilliam and Mrs Collins said simultaneously, and gave each other nervous smiles. The door slammed, the whip cracked and the two coaches rolled away, while the damp farewell party retreated with some relief into the shelter of the house – all except Mrs Collins, who, reopening her umbrella, prepared to return to the parsonage.

Colonel FitzWilliam volunteered to accompany her, and took charge of the umbrella. 'How is Miss Lucas?' he enquired, after they had walked some yards in silence.

Charlotte gave him a chilly glance.

'She and Mr Lawson are down at Wormwood End cottage, trying to comfort poor Mr Mynges. I had invited him to come and stay at the parsonage, but he would not. He said his place was with his friend – or where his friend had been – as long as it was possible for him to remain there. I believe there are still two days remaining before the expiry of his notice to quit,' she added drily.

'It was a bad business, a dreadful business,' said the colonel uncomfortably.

'Bad? It was atrocious!' Charlotte said sharply. 'That poor, poor man – driven to do such a thing.'

'You believe, then, that he did it on purpose?'

'Walk into a blazing bonfire? How could it have been an accident?'

'But he was blind.'

'He had the use of his other senses. He was an independent man, a man of strong feelings. He *knew* what he was doing, Colonel! I was down there at his house three days ago, talking to him. He said to me, "How can I be such a charge upon Ambrose? He has the task of finding another house for us, a house where I can learn my blind way about. Here it would not be so bad; I know every step and corner of Wormwood End. But at my time of life I am too slow to learn, too set in my ways to make the adjustment. I shall be nothing but a weight around his neck. I deserve to be cast out, like all those old frames and stretchers that he is burning outside in the garden." Finglow was a brave man, Colonel! I am only glad that Mr Collins was not here at the time,' she added, brushing an angry tear from her cheek.

'Why?' he asked incautiously.

'Mr Collins would have felt it his duty to be extremely disapproving. As it was, I thought that Mr Lawson, in his funeral sermon, did very well. He was tactful, friendly and discreet.'

'Lady Catherine was greatly surprised to hear what

a large number of Mr Finglow's friends came from London, besides all the local people.'

'Lady Catherine, perhaps, did well not to attend the funeral. And her absence, just now, will be no bad thing, until the matter has somewhat passed out of people's minds.'

'Yes, I suppose so. Perhaps the Delavals will soon leave. I rather hope so.'

'Oh? I thought they planned all sorts of surprises for Lady Catherine's return?'

He shrugged. 'Perhaps. I am not in their confidence.'

They had now reached the parsonage. Charlotte, taking the umbrella from him, said, 'Thank you for your escort, Colonel. Please say all that is friendly and condoling from me to Miss Anne. I shall come and see her soon, tell her.'

'Yes, of course,' said the colonel. He went on uncomfortably, 'I do not suppose—' caught Charlotte's indignant eye on him, muttered, 'Thank you, Mrs Collins,' and walked off forlornly into the rain.

VI

'A garden,' said Joss, 'be like a person.'

'What do you mean, Joss?'

'Well, look upon it this way. You don't give a care and help to someone, that body's a-going to turn agin you. Right?'

'I suppose so,' said Anne, thinking of herself. Nobody has given me much care and help, she thought, except Joss, to be sure. And I am against everybody. That is true.

'Leave your garden alone for two weeks,' pursued Joss, 'and that'll turn angry. And I don't mean just the weeds'll come up and start to plague you; no, the whole plot 'ull have a bad feel agin you. It'll turn sour, ye'll have to pamper and coddle a bit afore it'll welcome ye back.'

'Even a garden like this?' said Anne, looking across the

shaven lawns. 'Even a garden that doesn't belong to you?'

'That don't make no manner of difference. Just to have your name writ on a bit o' paper, that's no business of plants or trees. Is it? A garden belongs to the chaps as does the digging and pruning.'

'But Joss, don't you wish you had a garden of your own?'

'Some day I shall,' said Joss without impatience. 'I can wait. I'm planning. I've a flower book my ma left me. My garden'll have all the flowers that's in it. Bachelors' buttons, Canterbury Bells, sweet William, forget-me-nots, wallflowers, snapdragons.'

'Where is Pluto?' asked Anne, looking around and noticing the dog's absence for the first time.

'Didn't ye know? Lady Catherine had him done away with.'

'Done *away* with? *Pluto?*'

'Aye.' Joss reached down and tweaked a buttercup root out from between two hyacinth bulbs. 'Her eye lit on a pile of badger dung, out there on the grass, and she blamed Pluto. No use to tell her dogs 'on't eat hips and haws; she told Smirke to have him put down, and Smirke he told Muddle and Verity to see to it; so 'twas done. Time I was clearing out the lily pond; I allus shuts the dog in an empty stable stall those times, for he gets that excited in the water; you know how he is, Miss Anne—'

Joss spoke simply and without rancour, as if Pluto were still in being.

'What did they do?' Anne asked, trembling.

'Tied a stone round's neck and chucked him in the millpond, reckon; I didn't ask. Done's done.'

'I hate my mother.' Anne spoke with intense vigour. 'I really hate her. I hope she drowns on the way to Great Morran.'

'Now, Miss Anne! Ye must not feel so.'

'But I do! How can I help it?'

'What Lady Catherine does is her affair, not yours. And she will have to answer for it, surely. But your business, my deary, is to get quit of those viperous thoughts that's in ye, for they'll turn to gall and brimstone and eat away at ye and do ye all manner of harm. Look,' said Joss, and forked out another tussock of buttercup roots, 'ye do some of this work, dirty your hands a bit, turn yourself to do something worthwhile, and that'll ease your mind, wash all that blackness and bile out of ye.'

'I could pull up a whole meadow full of buttercups and I'd still hate my mother,' said Anne, nevertheless doing as he suggested.

'Drop the weeds in the trug here,' Joss directed. 'Don't scatter them abroad on the gravel-plat. I'll go to the tool shed and fetch a smaller fork for ye to use. That one there be a dandelion, ye have to go deep for him, his roots go down to Tartarus.'

'Good heavens, Joss, where did you learn about Tartarus? Was that one of the things Sir Felix told you?'

'Aye, he had a book about all they Greek gods and goddesses – ramshackle lot they were, simmingly,' said Joss, and went off whistling to the tool shed.

While he was gone, Smirke the head gardener came by, and paused to give Anne his toothy smile.

'Deary me, Miss Anne, what in the world would her ladyship say to see ye so clarted up and mucky, doing the garden-boy's work? What *would* she say?'

'Her ladyship is halfway to Exeter,' Anne said defiantly.

'And what about the gentleman, Colonel FitzWilliam? I doubt he'd not be best pleased to see ye – and that was a snowdrop ye just dug up.'

'I don't think the colonel would care in the least.'

Anne hastily thrust the snowdrop back into its earthy hole.

''Tis no fit occupation for a young lady.'

'I like doing it.'

'Well, well,' said Smirke indulgently, 'we mun see what the colonel has to say. Don't let Miss Anne tire herself now,' he told Joss, who came back at that moment with another hand fork. 'And you, boy, you see those lettuce seedlings are pricked out in the glass house afore this morning's past!'

''Tis a wonder he didn't send me off right away to cart muck,' said Joss, when Smirke had gone.

'I think,' said Anne, 'that Smirke encourages us to be friendly for – for reasons of his own.'

'Aye?' said Joss. 'What manner of reasons be those, do you think, Miss Anne?'

'So that later on he can ask me for money, and threaten otherwise to make a scandal. About us,' Anne said hardily.

Joss burst out laughing.

'"Are there no overgrown hedges,"' Mr Delaval read aloud from *The Gentleman's Magazine*, '"that rob you of hundreds of yards of ground, that might be cut in, and converted into firewood, pea-sticks, or rubbish to burn into manure? What if the hedge were cut close in, the walks made few and straight, no wider than three feet, and every inch of wall covered with something useful, or beautiful, or both?"'

'I am tolerably sure that my Aunt Catherine has no lack of firewood or pea-sticks,' remarked Colonel Fitz-William, 'And I do not believe that she would wish her walks to be reduced to three feet wide.'

Priscilla twitched the magazine away from her

brother and continued reading: '"I know from what I see, as I travel up and down the country, that there are few gardens, and especially those of the industrious classes, but might be made to produce double what they do, and everything of better quality!" But Ralph, you must admit that Lady Catherine's produce could hardly be bettered – those grapes and peaches equal anything that you might find in Mediterranean lands.'

'Of course, my dear, of course. But just listen to this: '"Are there no old and useless trees, that shut out the best of the morning sun, and prevent you from cropping to advantage some of the best ground you have? Are not your fruit trees overgrown, and many of them occupying ground for which their annual crops are no equivalent?" How about that? How about those great overgrown Spanish chestnut trees? And that huge, gross oak? I dare swear it is as much as twenty feet round the perimeter, and who needs all those acorns? It is not as if Lady Catherine kept pigs.'

'Sir Lewis de Bourgh was *particularly* fond of that tree,' Mrs Jenkinson put in timorously.

'Let me understand you, Mr Delaval,' said the colonel. 'Did my Aunt Catherine give you *carte blanche* to cut down and root up what you please of her timber and fruit trees? Is it such projects you had in mind when you promised her splendid surprises on her return?'

'Her ladyship has approved most magnanimously all my suggestions up to this time,' Mr Delaval countered. 'And her tastes in horticulture conform to mine in a highly gratifying degree.'

'Well,' suggested FitzWilliam, 'before you undertake the wholesale lopping of the timber in the park, or the uprooting of the knot-garden, or the felling of the apple orchard, I believe you should consult the feelings of my Uncle Luke, who was, after all, brought up in Hunsford Castle, which once occupied the site where this house now stands. He knew the garden from a boy – what gardens there were in those days. I think his opinion should be sought.'

'Oh, certainly, that's of course,' said Mr Delaval, 'but Lord Luke seems remarkably little interested in such matters.'

Coincidentally at that moment Lord Luke himself appeared, with dust on his cravat and his sparse grey locks somewhat disordered.

'Ah, there you are, my boy. Ring for Frinton and have him bring up a bottle of sherry, will you? I am as dry as an oast house. Those attics! Catherine must have had every shred of cloth, every scrap of paper, every splinter of wood that was housed in the old castle carried up there. And the light under the roof is abominable. There are but two windows. I have had Muddle and Verity transfer as many boxes as possible to an area where their contents may be inspected, but I misdoubt me it is going to be a task that will take many days, if not weeks . . .'

He rubbed his hands as if this prospect, on the whole, was an inviting one.

'But I need a helper.'

He looked hopefully at his four auditors, but their silence and expressions exhibited such a lack of intention to oblige him, that he sighed.

'Muddle and Verity?' suggested Colonel FitzWilliam. 'Having moved the boxes for you, would they not be the best—'

'Dear fellows, both of them, excellent in their way, most willing,' explained Lord Luke. 'But neither of them can read.'

'Perhaps my cousin Anne might be interested?'

Mrs Jenkinson looked scandalized.

'Grubbing about in the attics?' she said faintly. 'Surely no occupation for the Lady Anne?'

'Since she seems to spend most of her time just now grubbing about the flower borders with the garden-boy, I should have thought—'

'The garden-boy!' Lord Luke exclaimed. 'Can he read, I wonder?'

'I really have no idea.'

'You are sure you would not care to join me, Fitz?

Who knows what treasures of history may not be found up there?'

'My dear Uncle Luke, I would not for worlds deprive you of the pleasure of making such a dramatic historical discovery yourself.'

'But how will you pass your time here – if the task should take me several weeks?'

'What precisely is it that you are searching for, Uncle?'

'Oh – old school exercises and papers from my childhood. They are of no intrinsic value or interest to anybody except myself,' Lord Luke explained with an air of great unconcern.

'I see. Well, I shall be quite content strolling about the grounds, consulting with Mr Delaval about such improvements as he may think fit to put in hand – fishing in the lake, perhaps shooting a pigeon or two. Possibly Miss Delaval will honour me with her company from time to time in a game of croquet?'

'I am so sorry, I should have enjoyed that. But, unfortunately, my ankle . . .'

'Oh, of course, I had quite forgotten. Your ankle. And I imagine that will also prevent your furnishing any advice or assistance to Lord Luke in the attics?'

'*Most* unfortunately, yes!' She responded to Colonel FitzWilliam's look of slightly ironic enquiry with a display of her dimples.

‘I believe I saw a harp up there?’ Lord Luke pleaded. But he added fairly, ‘It had remarkably few strings.’

‘However many strings it had, I should have been unable to play it. My ankle . . .’

‘Yes, yes, of course. I wonder if that agreeable Miss Lucas could be persuaded to give me some assistance? She might be glad to escape, once in a while, from all the domesticity at the parsonage.’

‘Ask her by all means,’ shrugged FitzWilliam.

Frinton came in with the sherry and told Lord Luke:

‘My lord, there are two persons here from London, who both claim to have authorization from Lady Catherine to clean her diamonds. Were you cognizant of her ladyship’s intentions in the matter?’

‘Rundell and Bridge—’ began Mr Delaval, but Lord Luke interrupted him.

‘No, I am certain that my sister had the intention of hiring Gray’s of Sackville Street to do her business.’

‘Why not fetch down her maid?’ suggested Fitz-William. ‘She must have been in Aunt Catherine’s confidence.’

‘An excellent idea,’ said Lord Luke. ‘Let Pronkum be sent for, Frinton. And tell her to bring the gems. And show the men in here.’

‘Yes, my lord. And shan’t I let Anderson the footman

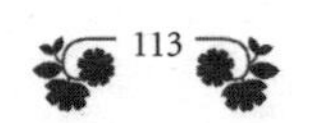

stand by the door while the persons are in here looking at the stones, sir, just to be on the safe side?'

'Not a bad notion, Frinton. For it does seem a trifle off that she sent for both men.'

'Do you think one of them is an *impostor*?' suggested Mrs Jenkinson, looking scared to death.

The two men were ushered in by Frinton, who announced: 'Mr Foster of Rundell's, Mr Bolton of Gray's – would you stand here, if you please,' as if he expected one or both of them to snatch up a porcelain dish or a silver snuffbox and make a bolt for it. Both men looked intensely respectable. Both were dressed in drab shopmen's ware of snuff-coloured broadcloth, and eyed each other combatively.

'I have a letter from a Mr Delaval, countersigned by Lady Catherine de Bourgh,' said Mr Foster.

'I have a letter from her ladyship *herself*,' said Mr Bolton.

Pronkum came in carrying an immense black jewel case and a look of extreme disapproval. She was a tall, bony woman with dyed black hair, a long face, high cheekbones and a highly coloured complexion.

'Well, well, Pronkum,' said Lord Luke. 'Can you explain this puzzle? To which of these establishments was Lady Catherine about to entrust her diamonds?'

'She hadn't yet decided,' said Pronkum, throwing a

sour look at the newcomers. 'She said, "Pronkum, I leave it to you. If you don't like the trim of either of them, you just keep a-cleaning the stones yourself, as you always have done, in lye made by soapy water, and brushing them with a brush of badger hair. You judge these gentry for yourself, Pronkum," says she, "and if you don't favour 'em, send them off with a flea in their ear." '

'Oh!' said Lord Luke, rather taken aback. 'Well, as you're here with the stones, let us take a look at 'em and hear what the fellers have to say. Frinton, why don't you lay a baize cloth over the tea-table and stand close at hand?'

Frinton did so, and Pronkum, showing considerable reluctance, drew a key from her reticule, unlocked the jewel case and then, with slow ceremony, laid out the jewels on the cloth: first the ear-bobs, then the brooches, then the tiara and finally the great three-strand necklace. Then, with even more reluctance, she stepped back from the table.

Everybody in the room was irresistibly drawn to the glittering display.

'*Don't touch!*' warned Pronkum sharply. '*Hands off!* Diamonds smear easy.'

'Humph,' said Lord Luke, peering short-sightedly. 'Well, gentlemen, what do you say? What price are you empowered to charge Lady Catherine for polishing up these sparklers? If I know my sister, she would go for the lowest bid!'

The two men drew near and cautiously inspected the gems. Then the man from Rundell's said:

'That's a big job. All those facets need polishing. Can't possibly be done here. I'd have to carry them back to town. And the price would be fifty pound. At the very least.'

His companion looked at him with utter scorn.

'Hark at him!' he said. 'The man's a gyp. He's a fleece. He's a sham! If he believes what he says, he don't know a diamond from a duck's egg. For a start, it would cost twice that figure to clean them, maybe three times. But in any case those stones are fakes. They are imitation. Ask *me*, I've been fetched down here on a fool's errand!'

Pronkum turned as white as rice-paper and dropped the jewel case.

VII

Letter from Miss Maria Lucas to Mrs Jennings

My dear madam,

Mr Collins has not yet returned to Hunsford. We learn that the drains at Longbourn Manor are in a shocking condition, and the house cannot be let until they are put in better order. (Mr Bennet, it seems, was a sad heedless householder who permitted many parts of his estate to fall into a parlous condition of neglect – my sister has had many communications from her husband lamenting this state of affairs.) By great good fortune Lady Catherine is away from home at this time, otherwise I am very sure she would never have permitted her incumbent clergyman to absent himself for so long.

As matters are, we go on very peacefully. At least in this

household. But now, dear ma'am, I have to relate to you a dreadful fatality which lately took place in this neighbourhood.

I told you in an earlier letter about the two painters who had been friends of Sir Lewis de Bourgh, and who for many years have occupied a house on the Rosings estate. And I also told you of the couple, Mr and Miss Delaval, who, due to a carriage accident, have been staying at Rosings House. Mr Delaval, who is most knowledgeable about improvements, and has a very persuasive manner, has been advising Lady Catherine on how best to perfect and develop her parkland and pleasure grounds, and she has been listening to him with a very willing ear. (The lime avenue is to go, I grieve to report, and the cherry orchard is to be grubbed up.) Mr Delaval's most recent piece of horticultural and aesthetic counsel related to the cottage where the two painters have been living for the past twenty-odd years. He persuaded Lady C. that it was a sad eyesore and should be pulled down, to make way for a grotto or a Grecian temple. She was most ready to comply with this advice, and gave the two friends one month's notice to quit. (Neighbourhood gossip has it that the two men, Mr Mynges and Mr Finglow, had been great friends of the late Sir Lewis de Bourgh and that Lady Catherine, who by all report was not on good terms with her husband, had disliked the two men on no better grounds than *because* they were favourites of Sir Lewis.) Lady C.'s edict was such a shock to the elder of the two men, Mr Finglow, who was already in a low state of health, that he suffered a severe seizure which rendered him blind; also, for two days, paralysed. Rousing from this latter condition he quitted the cottage, at a time when his friend was not at hand, tottered out of doors, and contrived to fall, or cast himself, into a great blazing bonfire composed of unwanted canvases, frames and articles of furniture, etc., which had been set burning not far distant from the house. From the shock and burns ensuing upon this accident, Mr Finglow soon succumbed after every possible measure to save him had been tried in vain, and his last rites were performed three days ago by the curate, Mr Lawson, attended by a very large concourse of people not only from the village and surrounding countryside, but also from town, for the two men were very popular. Lady Catherine and the Delavals did not attend the service, which may have been just as well, for I understand there is some local feeling against them. It is not greatly to be wondered at.

Lady C. is now gone into the West Country to visit her sister-in-law, the Duchess of Anglesea, who resides on an island off the Cornish coast, and the Delavals remain at Rosings until Miss D.'s ankle is mended, which seems to be a mighty slow business. Poor Miss Anne de Bourgh has been greatly distressed by the tragedy: she grows thinner daily and looks as if she cried her eyes out every night. Col. FitzWilliam does not seem able to comfort her. And Lady Catherine's brother, Lord Luke, though still resident at Rosings, is hardly to be seen (Mrs Jenkinson informs us), for he spends all the hours of daylight ensconced in the attics at Rosings, hunting for some document . . .

He asked me, very civilly, if I would assist him in sorting out papers from the hugger-mugger that is to be found up there. Apparently, when Hunsford Castle was torn down, all the contents and furnishings were stored in the barns of local farmers during the construction of the new mansion. When this was completed, the more valuable furniture was placed in the main salons (or some of it, at least; Lady C.'s taste inclining to lighter and more modern pieces than some of the massive and heavy, if historic, objects which had served her forebears), but anything in poor repair, or whose use was unknown, was relegated to the garrets, which run the whole length of the house under the tiles and above the servants' bedrooms. So there is an infinity of lumber, as indeed Charlotte and I observed, for she accompanied me up there to see what kind of a task Lord Luke was proposing for me. When she perceived the immense heaps of dusty anonymous objects, she cried out in horror and wholly forbade me to pass any time in such an unwholesome atmosphere, for, said she, if I did not breathe in enough dust to bring about my death from asphyxiation, I would assuredly meet my Fatal End due to some heavy object toppling on me from one of those ill-piled top-heavy mountains of Miscellaneous Rubbish.

Lord Luke was greatly cast down at hearing this prohibition, but indeed, Charlotte said later, it would be highly improper for me to be up there alone with Lord Luke (though as to that, I am sure he is the most harmless creature in the world), but Mr Collins, she said, would be shocked to death at the very notion, so it is not to be thought of. In a way I am sorry at missing the opportunity to delve in those amazing piles of odds and ends, for who knows what may not be there? Charlotte and I divert ourselves for hours together in concocting suggestions as to what may be the object of Lord Luke's search: I incline to King Alfred's diary, for portions of Hunsford Castle were Saxon in origin, but Charlotte's theory tends to a lost work by the author of *Beowulf*.

Thus we endeavour to comfort ourselves during what is, in truth, a sad enough time; for though we did not know Mr Finglow well, he was a man of such kindness and talent, and his end was so dreadful, that it has strongly affected the entire neighbourhood.

Col. FitzWilliam remains at Rosings still, for I understand that he has given his promise to escort Lord Luke back to Wensleydale when the latter has found what he is searching for and wishes to return home: but that may not be for some weeks yet, since both men, we understand, have promised Lady C. that they will remain in the house while she is absent. We do not see the colonel, he does not come to the parsonage any more and I am glad of it.

A mysterious story has been circulating in the village that two men came down from well-known London jewellers to inspect Lady C.'s diamonds and give an estimate for cleaning them, and that one of the men declared that the diamonds were counterfeit!

We hardly know what to believe! Lady C.'s maid, Pronkum, remains at Rosings and, it seems, is as astonished as anybody – indeed, she was quite prostrated.

Your affectionate friend,

Maria Lucas

'The dinner at Truro was disgusting,' pronounced Lady Catherine. 'And this road is abominable.'

'Yes, ma'am,' said Hoskins. 'Would your ladyship wish for a cup of tea from the flask?'

'Certainly not! I dare say it would be tepid, and would taste of nothing but the metal flask and sour milk. What time is it? Are we approaching Brinmouth? This stage seems to have lasted for ever.'

'I'm afraid, ma'am, I can't see the face of the carriage clock – the light is so poor. Would you wish me to stop the driver and step out into the road? It is likely to be lighter outside.'

'By no means. Let us get on as fast as may be. It would be lighter if it were not for this intolerable weather.'

'They told us at Launceston, ma'am, that they had had more rain in the last three days than in the last three months,' Hoskins said, compressing her lips as if such weather would never have been allowed in Kent.

'I do not believe it. I dare say one may always expect such weather in these parts. Where is the baggage coach? It seems to have been entirely left behind.'

Lady Catherine peered out disapprovingly at a dismal twilit vista of grey, hurrying clouds and windswept moorland set about here and there with large shapeless rocks.

'You may give me a dram of brandy, Hoskins – this road is so wretched and the coach sways about to such a degree that I feel quite queasy.'

'Yes, my lady.' No hint in the maid's manner suggested that she had been waiting for this moment since they left Truro. She unbuckled the strap around a hamper and brought out a silver hunting-flask, the top of which, when unscrewed, did service as a cup.

'There, ma'am.'

'You have hardly filled it more than half full.'

'Because the coach sways so, my lady.'

'Pour me another.'

'Certainly, ma'am.'

'Did you post the letter to Lord Luke that I gave you at Truro?'

'Of course, my lady.'

'I suppose he will not receive it for at least three days,' Lady Catherine said discontentedly. 'I cannot imagine why anybody chooses to live in such barbarous regions as these. And when I recollect that we still have a sea journey ahead of us . . .'

She yawned deeply once, and then again. The silver flask top slipped from her hand. Her head drooped sideways.

Hoskins neatly retrieved the flask top and screwed it back on to the flask. She surveyed her mistress attentively for some five or six minutes, then, satisfied, rapped on the hatch. When it opened:

'She's off!' the maid reported. 'Sleeping like a babby. Are we nearly there?'

'Just about. See those lights on up ahead? That be Brinton Tor; beyond lies the hill we gotta go down, and Brinmouth's at the foot. 'Tis a pesky steep hill, though; I'll not be sorry when we're down. Best you get out, my gal, and walk at the horses' heads, hold them back do they slip; this road's no better than a demmed waterfall.'

Grumbling and protesting at this extra duty, Hoskins nonetheless did as she was required. The horses slipped and stumbled and shivered; the coach swayed from side to side as they crept down the precipitous hill. On the left, a high bank rose into near-darkness; on the right, a steep declivity ran down to the lights of a town or village some distance below. Down there, the sea could be heard breaking on rocks, and there was also the sound of rushing water closer at hand.

Halfway down, the cause of this became apparent. The road surmounted a rude bridge spanning a swift-running body of water coming from the moorland above. The bridge consisted of no more than a single stone arch, without parapets. As the coach crossed this structure, a mass of branches and debris, which had collected against some obstacle in the stream above, suddenly broke free, and, with a loud crash, descended upon the vehicle. The horses slipped, staggered, broke their harness and fled on down the hill at a breakneck pace, cannoning against Hoskins, who fell into the ravine. The coach toppled over, hung against a bush for a moment, then plunged on down the hillside, until it finally came to rest, entangled in the boughs of a stunted tree, which grew on a bank at the confluence of two rushing streams.

The driver had been flung off his box and lay motionless on the bridge above.

By now it was almost completely dark.

'It is *so* kind of you, Colonel FitzWilliam, to give yourself the trouble of pushing me about the gardens,' sighed

Miss Delaval, turning her head in the wheelchair to give the colonel, who was propelling it, her most beguiling smile, accompanied by a gentle quiver of her thick dark eyelashes. 'My brother has been so wretchedly mortified by this unfortunate mishap that he is hardly to be seen just now, he keeps his room—'

'*Mishap?*' said the colonel, in a troubled voice. 'You refer to the death of Mr Finglow?'

'Oh! My dear sir, no!' Miss Delaval was shocked. 'No, that is not less than a *tragedy*! And Ralph does, of course, take himself most bitterly to task for ever having encouraged Lady Catherine in her whim to remove the cottage. If he had ever considered the possibility that it would lead to such a terrible outcome, he would naturally have scotched the plan when Lady Catherine first suggested it.'

'Oh? It was my aunt who first proposed that Wormwood End cottage be demolished?'

'But of course! It was her own idea entirely, from the very first! No, no, Ralph would never have suggested such a thing. He has far too much respect, indeed reverence, for art and artists, especially in the persons of those two talented protagonists. Well, it is no use to say two now, is it – that poor, poor Mr Mynges, what in the world, I wonder, will he do now? Move back to London, I dare say . . .'

FitzWilliam sighed, and said in a repressive tone, 'Well, at least he is no longer under notice to quit. My Uncle Luke and I persuaded Aunt Catherine's attorney that the notice was quite ineligible, and that he might remain in the cottage for whatever length of time he wished.'

'I dare say he will nonetheless wish to remove himself without too much delay. He cannot want to remain in a place with such awful association,' she suggested.

'Perhaps. But if *that* affair was not on your brother's mind, what mishap do you refer to that is causing him such mortification?'

Now the colonel's voice was tinged with irony.

'Why! I referred of course to the affair of the false jewellery! As you may recall, it was my brother who suggested summoning the man from Rundell and Bridge, and he now feels that he has made a fine fool of himself. He fears that when we return to London, his friends will have heard the tale and that he will be the butt of all the Mayfair clubs.'

'Oh? But they were not his jewels, after all. Why need he concern himself?'

'He feels, you see,' said Miss Delaval, twisting her head to a remarkable degree so as to fix her large, dark troubled eyes on the colonel, 'that Lady Catherine cannot have *trusted* him; that she perhaps had her real gems hidden away somewhere, awaiting her return . . .'

'Oh, I see. Is that what he thinks? It is true that my aunt is an unaccountable, devious character – on the surface she seems direct enough, even overbearing, but what governs her impulses one is not always able to guess.'

'And you, of *all* people, should know what motivates her,' said Miss Delaval in a rallying tone. 'Are you not her prospective son-in-law?'

'Possibly so. That issue depends on my cousin Anne.'

'Poor Miss Anne! She seems so utterly overset by these calamitous happenings,' sighed Miss Delaval. 'I have tried to lighten her spirits in every way that occurred to me – encouraging her to have a new trimming on her primrose muslin, and to try the effect of doing her hair in ringlets instead of that severe, Quakerish braided coronet she wears. But she turned on me almost with indignation, as if my efforts to cheer her mounted to a kind of heresy! And when Ralph asked her, only wishing to elevate her mind from what it continually dwells on, if she had any notion of some hiding-place where her mother might have secreted the real diamonds, so that, you know, he might have them furbished up against Lady Catherine's return, she rounded on him, positively like a wildcat. "Have you not done enough mischief here?" she cried at him. I have never seen him so repulsed! He quite crept away with his tail between his legs. I believe he has now offered his services to Lord Luke for that never-ending quest in the attics.'

'Perhaps,' suggested the colonel drily, 'Mr Delaval has some notion of coming across my aunt's diamonds in that quarter. But if that is his aim, I fear he is due for disappointment. Aunt Catherine has quite a detestation for that part of the house – any objects, indeed, that remind her of the old castle – and never sets foot there. I think it is the last place where she would deposit anything of value. It is far more probable that she took the real gems with her, to impress my Aunt Adelaide.'

'On a journey *overseas*, merely visiting her sister-in-law? Oh, no! Surely not!' Miss Delaval sounded outraged at the very possibility.

As the colonel and Miss Delaval approached the shrubbery, two figures emerged from it carrying baskets of cuttings.

'What a charming friendship that is, between Miss Anne and the garden-boy – what is his name? Joseph?' said Miss Delaval sweetly. 'At a time when poor Miss Anne is so low-spirited, it is a joy to see anybody who can bring her to a state of cheerfulness! I am sure it does one's heart good to hear her laugh.'

'Just so,' agreed the colonel, compressing his lips.

As the wheelchair passed the pair, deep in

horticultural discussion, Smirke approached from the other direction.

'You, Joss!' he said sharply, but with a hint of indulgence. 'His lordship was asking for you to go and help him shift a whole passel of stuff up in the attic. You'd best lay those cuttings to soak in a pail o' water.'

'I'll take care of them,' said Anne. 'I'll come with you, Joss, as far as the stable yard.'

'Ragwort's full as bad as buttercup,' FitzWilliam heard Joss telling Anne as they hurried off along the path. 'And did you know, there's a Sardinian herb that, they say, if you chew it, you die laughing!'

He and his companion burst into gales of chuckles.

'How delightful it is to hear them!' said Miss Delaval.

Colonel FitzWilliam frowned, and accelerated the pace of the wheelchair.

Mrs Collins and her sister Maria were visiting Ambrose Mynges at Wormwood End. Alice the cat, who treated most visitors with haughty suspicion, had taken a fancy to Maria, and came to rub against her. Mr Willis the apothecary was there also, advising Young Tom about his sleep problem.

'Cold water and vinegar,' he was saying. 'Sponged over the brow, last thing at night.'

'I detest the smell of vinegar,' said Ambrose.

'Camomile tea,' suggested Charlotte. 'Or hops, passion-flower, lemon verbena, basil, violet leaves – and of course catnip. The catnip leaves should be steeped, but not boiled, and flavoured with honey.'

'Mrs Collins is a better physician than I shall ever be,' said Mr Willis.

'Good friends who come and chat are the best friends of all.'

'We have brought you a basket of dried cherries,' Charlotte said. 'Besides being so delicious, I find they are very soothing if chewed slowly, last thing at night.'

'Cherries are also sovereign for gout,' said Mr Willis. 'I always prescribe fifteen cherries a day, fresh or dried, for all my gout patients.'

'*Grief*, not gout, is what ails me.'

'We know. We know that,' Charlotte told him compassionately. 'And if there were anything more we could do, you have only to ask. If you cared to come and stay at the parsonage—'

'You are an angel of goodness, Mrs Collins, but there is nothing more that you can do. I prefer to stay here, where I feel near to my friend.'

Willis took one of the dried cherries and ate it.

'Excellent,' he said. 'I recognize the flavour. Are they not made from Mrs Godwin's receipt?'

'Indeed, yes,' said Charlotte. 'I have her kitchen book

and use it faithfully. Every year I take care to get a great sackful from the Rosings cherry orchards – dear me, I suppose next year I must look further afield, if the orchards are to be cut down. That is such a pity, is it not? Those trees provide a handsome crop, year after year.'

'Perhaps, now this cottage is to be spared, Lady Catherine will have second thoughts about the lime avenue and cherry orchard also.'

'Sir Lewis was particularly attached to that orchard,' remarked Mr Willis, shaking his head. 'Many an evening I used to see him walking there as I drove by, especially when the trees were in bloom. And in his will, when he died, it was found that he had expressed a wish that a sack of the cherries should be delivered, each year, free, to Mr Godwin, who was then the incumbent here, for the use of his wife.'

'Very touching – very thoughtful of him.'

'Only, as it happened, Mrs Godwin predeceased Sir Lewis, so the bequest was not carried out. But I suspect we are tiring Mr Tom. I think it is time I took my departure.'

Mr Willis rose, bowed to the ladies and walked outside to where his cob stood patiently waiting.

'Did you know Sir Lewis well, Mr Mynges?' Maria was suddenly moved to ask Young Tom.

'I? No, not well. At least, not so well as my – as my

friend Desmond. D-Desmond had been coming here for a number of years before I knew him. He and Sir Lewis had been at school together. Why do you ask, Miss Lucas?'

'I – oh, I just wondered what – what sort of a man Sir Lewis was. One receives such conflicting accounts of a person who has died, does one not? I wondered, for instance, if he was fond of poetry.'

'*Poetry?* Why do you ask that?'

'Oh, a person who chooses to wander in a blossoming cherry orchard must surely have poetic leanings in them, do you not think?'

'Maria, you are letting your fancy fly away with you,' said Charlotte. 'And it is time we returned to those four hungry children. Goodbye, Mr Mynges, we will come again soon.'

'You cannot come too often,' he said.

On the way back to the parsonage, Maria was unwontedly silent. She was thinking about a handwritten poem which she had discovered in Mrs Godwin's kitchen book. It had been tucked inside some voluminous instructions for dealing with a chimney fire ('Close all doors and windows tightly, then procure a wet blanket . . .'). The writing was not that of Mrs Lucy Godwin, who had herself transcribed many of the receipts in a small, neat hand. This was larger and more flowing. Maria remembered the poem, which had been written on a small piece of paper, perhaps torn out of a diary or notebook:

Muslin, not silk
White as new milk
The canopy spreads
Over our heads
Delicate mist
Shelters our tryst
Softer than lace
Pale as thy face.
Blossoms must pass
Scatter on grass
Cherries instead
Glowing and red
Cluster above
Speak of our love . . .

Not the world's greatest poem, certainly, yet Maria found something touching and straightforward about it. She wondered who had written it. She did not mention it to Charlotte.

'A letter from Lady Catherine at last!' exclaimed Mrs Jenkinson, hurrying with it into the breakfast parlour.

Lord Luke looked up in surprise.

'Not from Great Morran, surely? She cannot have travelled as far as that already? Or at least,' he added, recollecting himself, 'if she had, a letter could not so soon have returned from there?'

'No, this was sent from Truro. She complains about the food and the weather. Both atrocious. And hopes that you are in good health, Lord Luke.'

'Well, I am *not*,' he said peevishly. 'My old trouble is come upon me, I dare say thanks to all that dirt and dust upstairs. But I was never one to complain.'

Mrs Jenkinson showed in a look her disbelief of this statement, but was too well trained to utter anything more than a sympathetic sigh.

The garden-boy, Joss, was announced, and came in looking dusty but cheerful.

'Well, Joss, how goes it?'

'You said to bring you boxes o' papers, me lord, so here's one I found. 'Tis all full of a mort of written stuff. I brought it to ye directly.'

Mrs Jenkinson uttered a slight scream.

'The dust! Fetch a kitchenmaid, Frinton, with a duster, and let her wipe some of that dirt off before it spreads all over the room.'

'Oh, never mind *that*!' Lord Luke impatiently exclaimed. 'Let's have a look – here, I'll flap a table napkin over it.' He did so, producing clouds of thick snuffy powder which caused everybody in the room to cough and sneeze.

Lord Luke, meanwhile, was delving with excited hands among the yellowing and brittle papers in the mahogany coffer.

But after a very short time he gave up in disgust.

'It's naught but a confounded *novel*! By Mrs Ophelia Ogilvie – never heard of the woman.'

'Oh, but I have!' cried Mrs Jenkinson, displaying great interest. 'I believe she was a great-aunt of Sir Lewis and a great friend of Walpole. She wrote a number of novels, but only one was ever published.'

'I'm not surprised to hear that, for this one looks devilish dull,' said Lord Luke. 'Do you want to read it, Mrs Jenkinson? Take it then, it's yours . . . No, boy, no, Joss, I fear that is not the object of my researches. Back to your labours . . . If you find the papers I want, I shall reward you with ten gold guineas.'

'Thank 'ee, my lord.' Joss grinned, touched his dusty forelock and disappeared through the folding doors.

VIII

When Lady Catherine recovered consciousness, it was to find herself in a stuffy, scantily furnished place, lying on what felt like an exceptionally hard and hummocky couch. She felt hideously unwell – an unusual and unwelcome state for Lady Catherine, who, all her life, had enjoyed excellent health, so much so that the sting of a bee or a touch of indigestion were the severest ills she had ever suffered. Now her bones ached, she seemed to be covered with bruises and abrasions from head to foot, a hammer beat inside her skull, and yet, despite these various afflictions, she was consumed by ravenous hunger.

'Where am I?' she said aloud, expecting an instant response. But none came. She tried to move. But the effort cost her such an assault of pain in every portion of her anatomy that once more she lost consciousness.

This second faint passed into a more normal slumber from which she presently awoke, and once more called out, 'Where am I? Who is there?'

Still she received no answer.

At last, with an immense effort, she pushed herself upright into a sitting posture, and looked about her.

She had been, she now discovered, lying in a ship's hammock made of rope netting. She had been covered with the sable travelling cloak that she had brought with her in the coach, and her head had been pillowed on the matching sable muff. Both these articles were exceedingly wet and mud-caked.

With extreme difficulty, for she was still excessively weak, she managed to push herself out of the hammock and stand up on stiff and trembling legs.

'Hollo there!' she called. 'Where am I? What has happened? Hoskins! Thompson! Where are you? Where is this?'

Nobody answered.

With growing alarm and astonishment, Lady Catherine began to take stock of her circumstances.

She was in a small room which was both cold and damp. Not surprisingly: for she now began to realize, what she had first taken for a feverish rumbling inside her own skull was, in fact, the surge of waves beating on a rocky coast somewhere close at hand, and as well as that, she seemed to hear the continuous booming of a torrent, or waterfall.

The room she was in had windows, but they were small and high, and offered nothing but squares of dim light. There was also a door, made of solid, unpainted wood. Lady Catherine tottered towards it and attempted to open it, but it was locked. She beat on it with her fists and called, 'Open this door! Open up, I say!' but there was no response.

She noticed that a pool of water had collected inside the door, and more seemed to be coming from the crack under it.

Now Lady Catherine began to be very frightened.

I am imprisoned, she thought. Who can have done this? What can their intentions be?

She tried to remember what had happened, but her memory failed her. She had been in the coach with Hoskins; they had stopped at Truro and had a very disagreeable meal of mutton stew and overcooked vegetables. Then what had ensued? She could recall nothing more.

Turning to take stock of the place where she found herself, she received a shock.

For she heard a loud male snore, and discovered that there was a man lying motionless, apparently fast asleep, on a mattress on the floor in one corner of the room.

He was a bearded, grizzled individual with long white hair and very shabby clothes which were soaked with water and caked with mud – like her own gown and pelisse, Lady Catherine now observed. She and that man must have been together somewhere. Had there been some kind of accident?

'Wake up!' she said to him urgently. 'Wake up and tell me what has happened!'

But he slept on, and, even when she shook him, did not respond at all. Now she began to suspect that he might be ill – his colour was high and his breathing rapid and stertorous.

'Hollo! Ho!' she called at the door again. 'This man is unwell. I believe he needs a doctor.'

But no answer came, and she began to have the horrible feeling, not that there were hostile people beyond the door who had no intention of replying, but that nobody was near at hand at all; that she and this sick stranger were cast away in some wilderness where they might die of hunger or cold without the least chance of succour.

Once more Lady Catherine surveyed the room in which she found herself – and this unknown man – now simply with a view to what amenities it offered.

The walls were of stone, and the floor of beaten earth. Nails had been hammered into beams in the walls and on these a few male garments hung – also one or two cooking utensils, a long-handled pot, a skillet, a wooden spoon. A blackened side of bacon dangled from a beam in the roof. A large pile of apples lay in a corner, many of them rotten. From a spout in one wall water trickled down into a small stone bowl, and then away through a drain that led under the wall. The floor sloped slightly downwards to the corner containing this drain. Three slabs of granite in the centre of another wall formed a fireplace, but the hearth held only dead ashes. There was a woodpile, however, in the corner opposite the apples. A narrow shelf held a lamp and two tallow candles.

The pool of water just inside the door was growing larger.

Lady Catherine began to realize that any hope of succour, fire, or food for herself and this stranger might depend entirely on her own efforts – and she had never lit a fire in her life.

Colonel FitzWilliam had wheeled Priscilla Delaval in her basket-chair across the park to Hunsford churchyard to lay flowers on the grave of Desmond Finglow. The grave was turfed over, but as yet no headstone had been erected.

Hunsford church, tiny, grey and ancient, crouched against the side of a hill between two majestic cypress trees. The neighbourhood was so small that hardly a score of headstones occupied the graveyard. The most recent one, not far removed from Old Tom's grave, recorded the deaths of Barnabas Goodwin, late rector of the parish and canon of Canterbury, and his dear wife Lucy, who had predeceased him by a number of years.

'Why is there no tombstone for Sir Lewis de Bourgh?' enquired Miss Delaval, after she had laid her bunch of sweet-scented narcissi, hyacinths and hawthorn blossom on Old Tom's grave. 'Are they not beautiful? I asked Smirke to prepare me a choice bouquet. He is such a kind, willing, obliging man, is he not? I find his conversation most entertaining.'

'Kind and willing to *some*,' said Colonel FitzWilliam with reserve. 'There is no stone out here, Miss Delaval, because there is a memorial tablet to Sir Lewis inside the church commemorating his various excellent qualities. Would you care to go inside and take a look at it?'

'Oh, no, thank you, it is much more pleasant out here. Yes, now I recollect seeing it at Sunday service – erected by his sorrowing widow, was it not? I wonder just how sorrowing some of these widows really are, do not you, Colonel FitzWilliam? I assume it is quite a number of years since Lady Catherine left off her black crape and bombazine?'

'Do you care to return to the house?' suggested the colonel. 'The sky is clouding.'

'Oh, no, let us remain here a little longer. The view is so agreeable, up that slanting hillside, with the dark clouds and the young green of the trees and white thorn blossom – I wish poor Mr Mynges would do one of his delightful paintings of it. I wish he were here to observe it with us.'

The colonel looked as if he shared this wish.

'Tell me, Colonel,' enquired Miss Delaval, 'why are you so resolved on marrying your cousin Anne? If you will permit me to say so, neither yourself nor your intended bride appear to have the least inclination for the match. And surely – forgive me! – your own circumstance cannot be so very moderate as to compel you to this course?

'I know, I know, you think me shockingly impertinent to put such a question to a gentleman whom I have known only since we met at Mr Bingley's house. But as my brother is such a *great* friend of Mr Bingley, and I understand you have known Mr Bingley for ever, I consider that I am entitled to rush in where angels fear to tread!'

She gave him an arch smile.

'The reasons for the connection are numerous and – and are the concern of several people besides myself,' replied the colonel in his most grave and guarded manner. 'By no means all of them are – are economic.'

'In other words, the family have decided that your poor cousin Anne will never be off the shelf unless you take pity on her. And yet,' pursued Miss Delaval thoughtfully, 'she is not so very plain. I have seen her sometimes, when the poor dear is not on her best behaviour (or should I say her worst?), look quite lively and engaged. When my brother succeeds in getting her to pay attention to one of his jokes, for instance. Oh, if only *I* were a married lady and could bring her out for a season in town, I have not the least doubt that she might be most creditably established. It is really her unfortunate relationship with her mother that is the root cause of the mischief. Only remove her from Lady Catherine, and what a change might be effected!'

'You suggest, for instance, that she should marry your brother?' the colonel said drily.

'Well, it would be for the benefit of both, would it not? Miss Anne would lead a much more entertaining and varied life with Ralph than if she were to remain here at Rosings for the rest of her days – and *you* would be free of an onerous duty! I wonder what use you would make of your freedom?' (Another airy smile.) 'Shall I undertake a guess?'

Her question remained unanswered, for at this

moment the dark grey cloud which had been the object of Miss Delaval's admiration suddenly discharged its contents in the form of a heavy shower.

Neither Miss Delaval nor the colonel were dressed for such a contingency, since they had set forth in bright sunlight; he therefore made haste to wheel her wicker chariot into the shelter of the church porch.

'Gracious me! How very abrupt that came on! It shows how engrossing our conversation must have been that we did not observe the cloud approaching. But I always *do* feel so very much at ease with you, Colonel – our minds seem to march together so freely, have you noticed that? I sometimes feel as if we had known each other in a previous existence. Do you believe in the transmigration of souls, Colonel?'

'Certainly not! Shall we go into the church?'

'Oh, no, let us not. Somebody is playing the organ in there. And I dare say this shower will not last so very long. While we wait, you can do me a kindness, Colonel – I seem to have got a thorn in my finger. It must have been from the may blossom in that posy. Can you possibly extract it for me? You will have to squeeze it out with your finger and thumbnail. Can you see it?'

FitzWilliam was not sure that he could.

'The light is so bad. Had you not best wait until we

return to the house? I am sure Mrs Jenkinson will be able to get it out with hot water and a pair of tweezers.'

'But it is so painful! Do please try! If you knelt down you could look at it more closely.'

The colonel's expression suggested that he did not relish this task. The church porch was a large one, spacious enough to accommodate the basket-chair. It was floored with stone flags, which were both damp and muddy. Plainly regretting the deleterious effect of these on his pantaloons, the colonel crouched down, took Miss Delaval's hand in both his own and attempted to squeeze out the hawthorn splinter.

It was at this moment that Charlotte Collins and her husband, equipped with a pair of umbrellas, came hastening through the churchyard to rescue Maria Lucas, who had been playing the organ inside the church. And, simultaneously, Maria herself came out of the church into the porch.

'I found a funny thing in the attics,' Joss told Anne.

'What was that?'

Anne could never have enough of hearing Joss's description of the extraordinary old articles that rusted and mouldered away up in the attics of Rosings House: sabres, spits, chain mail, crossbows, warming-pans, ancient crumbling pieces of parchment containing who knew what journals, diaries, outdated information. Books; pictures; moth-eaten garments.

'It is like having a millstone – like a whole houseful of millstones – up there, weighing down whoever lives in the house,' said Anne. 'If Rosings belonged to me, I would fling it all out.'

'Won't it belong to you by and by, missie, when you weds the colonel?'

'I don't want to wed him,' said Anne. 'And I am certain he doesn't want to wed me. I believe he would like to marry Maria Lucas – I'm sure he loves her.'

'Why don't he speak for her, then?'

'She has no money. And he is promised to me. When he and I are married, all Rosings will be his, he will be rich enough then. I wonder if he will want to keep all that rusty rubbish in the attics?'

'Why don't you ask him these things?'

'I don't wish to talk to him. I don't like him enough. But what was it, Joss, that you found up there?'

'Why,' said Joss, 'it was a book. A book of trees. *Talking About Trees*.'

'What is so odd about that?'

'Naught in itself. But – well, I'd have to show you. 'Twas in a chest of books and papers I fetched down to the library to show his lordship. I reckon 'tis there yet.'

'I'll go and find it,' said Anne, 'and bring it here.'

The two friends were planting out seedlings in a potting shed at the far end of the great walled vegetable garden.

'Wait there, I shall not be many minutes,' said Anne. 'What did the book look like?'

''Twas bound in red leather, Miss Anne. But very faded. And only a little book – no bigger than a half-brick.'

Anne nodded and ran off. But when she reached the library, she found there a scene of dismay and shock. Lord Luke was in the room, and Colonel FitzWilliam, Mrs Jenkinson, Frinton the butler, the Delavals and Lady Catherine's maid Pronkum, who was having a fit of hysterics, weeping and laughing and calling upon heaven to have mercy.

'Oh, be quiet, woman, will you! Cease making that atrocious racket!' cried Lord Luke with furious impatience.

'What in the world is the matter?' asked Anne, startled out of her usual reserve.

'Matter? Butchery and bloodshed's the matter!' shrieked Pronkum. 'And torture and dreadfulness and wicked shockingness!'

She beat her hands frantically on a bundle of documents that lay on the library table. Presumably they had come from the attics, for they emitted a cloud of dust.

Mrs Jenkinson and Miss Delaval attempted to hush Pronkum, while Anne asked again, 'What is the matter?'

'Your uncle has had a letter,' said Colonel FitzWilliam, who was looking very pale and grave.

'A letter? From whom?'

'Oh, my lady, my lady!' shrieked Pronkum.

Anne was bewildered.

'Is the letter from my mother?'

'Oh, dear Lord Luke!' cried Mrs Jenkinson anxiously.

'Do you think it right that Miss Anne should know about this?'

'She has reached the age of reason,' snapped Lord Luke. 'She is eighteen, is she not?'

'Is my mother dead?' enquired Anne.

'No, no. At least, we hope not,' said Colonel Fitz-William.

'If she is not dead, what has happened?'

'The letter is unsigned,' said Lord Luke. 'It appears to come from Cornwall, or somewhere in the West Country. It demands money for the return of your mother, and makes alarming threats if the money is not paid.'

'How much money? And what sort of threats?'

Lord Luke and FitzWilliam exchanged looks.

'No precise sum is stated,' Lord Luke told Anne, his severe expression suggesting that he found her behaviour far too undaughterly, composed and matter-of-fact. 'Nor are the threats in any way specific. They merely state that great harm and punishment will be inflicted upon my poor sister if the moneys are not paid over.'

'But how can they be paid, if no particular sum is stated? Or place of payment?'

'The letter intimates that another communication will follow later.'

'I believe,' put in Mr Delaval, 'that in such cases of kidnapping this is a customary procedure, so as to heighten alarm and despondence, you know, in the unfortunate relatives of the kidnapped person.'

Lord Luke and Colonel FitzWilliam glanced at him sharply, manifesting disapproval at his claiming such familiarity with the niceties of kidnapping procedure.

'May I see the letter?' said Anne, stretching out her hand to Lord Luke, who held a grimy and much-folded piece of paper.

He appeared hesitant. 'I am not sure if it will be proper – some of the expressions employed are very coarse.'

'Oh, good gracious!' Anne said irritably. 'She is my mother.'

But as Lord Luke, capitulating, was about to pass over the paper, Pronkum, with a loud scream, snatched it and flung it into the fire.

'That is the only place for such a wicked message!' she cried, and, casting herself full-length on the floor, drummed with her feet and sobbed at the top of her voice.

'Oh, fetch a couple of footmen, Frinton, and take her upstairs,' said Lord Luke in disgust. 'Let us have a little peace around here.'

'But what can be done about my mother?'

'Why – nothing, now. Not,' said Lord Luke scrupulously, 'that we could have taken any practical measures, even had we retained that paper.'

'We could have shown it to the constables,' pointed out Colonel FitzWilliam.

Lord Luke's expression showed how little help he felt this measure would have provided. Mrs Jenkinson – since Anne declined any restoratives, smelling salts, or condolences, hastened away to help the housekeeper pacify Pronkum, whose shrieks could still be heard ringing through the house.

'Poor Miss Anne!' said Priscilla Delaval. 'This must come as a severe shock to you.'

'Well,' Anne said dispassionately, 'it is not often that one receives such a piece of news, I suppose.'

She glanced into a box of faded, dusty books that stood on a side-table, and, selecting the one she was seeking, took it out and left the room.

But when she returned to the potting shed, Joss was no longer there.

Smirke was there instead, busy stirring an evil-smelling mixture of rainwater and hop manure.

'I was obliged to send the lad off to Marsden for a cartload of potash, Miss Anne,' he said smoothly. 'Young Joss can't always be at your beck and call, you know. Or I should be obliged to tell his lordship how much time you spend with him.'

'I doubt if his lordship would care,' Anne said coldly. But she gave Smirke a guinea and carried the book, *Talking About Trees*, back to her own bedroom.

Inside the cover was an inscription in faded brown ink:

A Mon Chéri
from
His Fair Star

and under the inscription were four lines of verse in the same hand:

O eat your cherries, Mary
O eat your cherries now
O eat your cherries, Mary
That grow upon the bough.

Lady Catherine was relieved to find what she took to be

a tinderbox in a small canvas bag on the shelf with the tallow candles. It was a kind of pistol mechanism in which, by turning a wheel, a flint was made to strike a steel plate. Unfortunately it took her a great many efforts before she managed to make it strike a spark, and then her lack of dexterity was a shocking hindrance, for even when she achieved a spark, she could by no means persuade it to ignite the strips of charred linen and rope ends dipped in pitch, which were presumably intended to be used as kindling material. She tried and tried, and could have wept with frustration, remembering the high-piled fires and the closed Rumbury stoves which burned day and night at Rosings. Did the kitchen fire ever go out? If it did, Lady Catherine knew nothing of the process by which some kitchenmaid or scullion persuaded it to blaze up again.

At last, more by luck than skill, she did succeed in producing a tiny, flickering frame. No paper was to be seen, but she remembered that in her muff she had retained a scrap left over from the letter home she had despatched from the inn at Truro. Delving into the pocket of the muff, she was relieved to find that it was tolerably dry inside, and that the paper was still there and still combustible.

With trembling hands she enclosed the little flame in a framework of twigs and shavings scraped from among the logs, and felt a surpassing sense of triumph when she succeeded in creating a small but healthy blaze, which she carefully augmented with all the driest bits of wood that she could find in the heap. The warmth was most gratifying, and so was the light.

Lady Catherine had no idea what time of day it was, for she wore no watch, and the travel clock had been left behind in the carriage.

So far, so good. The fire was a comfort, but she was, by this time, so hungry that she felt weak and sick. She ate an apple. It was sour, but quenched her thirst and helped allay the worst pangs of hunger. She eyed the flitch of bacon – but it was out of her reach. There was a three-legged stool, but Lady Catherine was not going to venture herself standing on *that*. She still suffered from the intermittent spells of dizziness. If only the wretched man would wake up!

'Sir! Sir! You!' she addressed him urgently. 'Rouse yourself!'

But he snored on, and she was bound to admit to herself that his forehead and cheeks looked flushed and hot; his sleep was not natural slumber, but that of fever.

And all that the miserable cabin contained was apples and an inaccessible side of bacon!

There was, however, a cooking-pot, and there was a

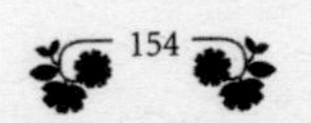

knife. And there was water. Grimly, Lady Catherine set to work, clumsily chopped up half a dozen apples, using the stool as a chopping board, and set them to boil in the pot with some water. She hoped by this process to make a kind of apple porridge.

The process took much longer than she had expected. She burned herself several times until she discovered how to wrap her hand in a layer of petticoat before touching the handle of the pot. Her petticoats, of which she had put on numerous layers for the journey, were otherwise a decidedly bulky inconvenience, since all her tasks had to be performed at ground level.

When the apple sludge was prepared, she set the pot on the earth floor to cool and levered herself into the hammock again, for all these efforts had exhausted her. The fire would burn for an hour or two yet: she had built it up with several substantial logs. Perhaps some deliverer would presently arrive . . .

She slept.

Mr Stillbrass, Lady Catherine's attorney, was summoned from Tunbridge Wells and came in haste.

When told that the ransom note had been burned, he looked exceedingly grave.

'That was a most injudicious thing to do!'

'It was an accident. Lady Catherine's maid was

distraught. But in any case, there was no signature, no means of identifying the writer.'

'You did not recognize the handwriting?'

'The note was printed – very clumsily printed,' Fitz-William recalled. 'It seemed like the scrawl of a low-class, illiterate person.'

'Oh, my poor dear sister!' lamented Lord Luke. 'I hope she is not fallen into the hands of some blackguards or ruffians who will villainously mistreat her!'

Anne reflected that these were the kindest sentiments she had heard her uncle express towards her mother for some considerable time.

'And you have not, since that one, received another note?'

'No, we have not.'

Lord Luke seemed rather puzzled and surprised at this. But he added, 'Doubtless the villains wish, by prolonging and heightening our anxiety, to render us more amenable to some outrageous ransom demand. What kind of sum, Mr Stillbrass, do you think may be required of us?'

'I suppose that must depend on the class of persons who have committed this felony. If they are, as you say, low-class ruffians, their demands may not be so very exorbitant. A sum such as five hundred pounds may be the summit of their expectations.'

'If they are better educated, you think they may expect more?' FitzWilliam said ironically. 'What can we afford to defray, out of my aunt's estate? Yes, cousin Anne, you may well look grave – whatever the sum may be, it must all come out of your dowry!'

'I assure you, cousin,' Anne told him coldly, 'that my thoughts ran in quite another direction.'

She said to Mr Stillbrass, 'Sir, since you are here, I think it must be proper to hand over to you this copy of my father's will, which J— which was discovered up in the attics among some other papers of my father's, during my Uncle Luke's researches up there.'

Mr Stillbrass was electrified.

'A will? Another will of your father's? God bless my soul! What next? What is its date? I must pursue it most carefully. If it should post-date the one that has been implemented – good heavens, good heavens!'

She handed him the document, which, like all the papers, deeds and records fetched down from the attics, was in poor condition – yellowed, crumbling and dusty. Mr Stillbrass's expression, when he studied it, was one of relief.

'No, this is the same testament, of the same date, that I have in my office. The date, the bequests, are the same. Thank heaven!' He turned the pages. 'No, here is a codicil – this I do not have. It is handwritten in your father's hand, unwitnessed, though, therefore invalid.'

'What are its provisions?' Colonel FitzWilliam asked with interest.

'There is only one. "My cottage in Wales – Uthan, at Moel-y-Fiediog, to my eldest child." Well, that is you, Miss Anne. You were Sir Lewis's only child, therefore his eldest. You would have inherited the cottage, on your majority, without his troubling to add the codicil.'

'I never knew that my father owned a cottage in Wales.' Anne was quite startled. 'I did not know that he had even been to Wales. My mother has never mentioned such a property.'

'It was a whim – he purchased it quite late in his life. I do not believe that he visited it above two or three times. A smallholder's dwelling, you know, with two or three acres of grazing, no more. I hardly think it would suit your tastes, Miss Anne!'

'Who is in it now?'

'Nobody. It was let to an old shepherd but he, I think, died some years ago. Nobody else has come forward as a prospective tenant. It stands too remote.'

'When we are married,' FitzWilliam said in a kindly tone to Anne, 'we will make a journey into Wales to look at the property, and decide what is to be done with it.'

Anne gave him a cold glance.

'I am obliged to you, cousin. But meanwhile, what is

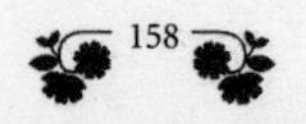

to be done about my mother? Could we not advertise in the press?'

Mr Stillbrass looked at her with some surprise and some respect.

'You have a head on your shoulders, Miss Anne! But do we really wish her predicament to be made public?'

Lord Luke and Colonel FitzWilliam were both firmly against this suggestion.

Lord Luke said: 'No, no, that would be to bring down a dozen impostors and charlatans on our heads, all threatening – or promising – to produce her in return for outrageous sums of ransom. No, our only recourse is to keep silent, let no one know that there is anything amiss and wait until we receive a second message.'

'I believe you are in the right of it, Lord Luke,' Mr Stillbrass acknowledged, though he seemed a trifle scandalized at the matter-of-fact way in which Lord Luke laid plans to deal with his sister's abduction.

Colonel FitzWilliam said: 'My Aunt Adelaide in Great Morran was, so far as we know, expecting her sister-in-law for a visit. Presently she will be writing to ask why Aunt Catherine has not arrived. What should we do then?'

'I will advise you when that happens. I shall be in constant touch, never fear,' said Mr Stillbrass, and took his leave.

'Prosy old ass!' said Lord Luke. 'Anne, my dear, will you send for Joss? I may as well continue with my researches. And my old trouble forbids my passing any more time in those villainously dusty attics.'

Letter from Miss Maria Lucas to Mrs Jennings

My dear madam,

Mr Collins is at last come back into Kent, but my sister Charlotte has begged me to remain here at Hunsford parsonage for some weeks yet, as Lady Catherine is gone off to visit her sister-in-law, the Duchess of Anglesea, and, lacking her rule up at Rosings House, Mrs Jenkinson and the housekeeper come at all times asking Charlotte's advice, so she is glad to have help with the children.

Mr Collins has let Longbourn Manor to a Captain Price, and seems very well satisfied with his tenant, who will be at sea most of the time, but who is an active, capable and sensible young man. Mr C. is somewhat dismayed to find Lady Catherine gone from home, as he has a great regard for her and hardly knows how to go on when she is not at hand to give him his instruction. (By the bye, it seems there is some mystery about Lady C.'s whereabouts. We at the parsonage are not supposed to know about this, it is kept a secret up at Rosings, but the news leaked out through Smirke the head gardener whose mother, Mrs Smirke, lives in Hunsford village and comes up to do the heavy laundry at the parsonage. Smirke, says Mrs S., received a letter which he was to hand to Lord Luke; this letter did not come through the post but passed from hand to hand. What the contents were we do not know, but we surmise that it related in some way to Lady C.'s whereabouts, for Col. FitzWilliam's valet, a very well-set-up young man who is a nephew of my sister's housekeeper Mrs Denny, avers that a letter came to his master from the latter's aunt, the Duchess of Anglesea, enquiring why Lady C. had not yet arrived to visit her as expected. She, the duchess, is much distressed at this, for she lies sick abed and nigh to her end, so was wishful for her sister's company. All this is a great enigma, which has us quite in a puzzle.)

Meanwhile, affairs in this neighbourhood go on much as before. Poor Mr Mynges the painter is still in his cottage, Wormwood End, for since Lady Catherine's departure his notice to quit has been withdrawn. Charlotte and I go to visit him and take him small comforts. He is a very gentle, sincere man; not, I think, such a gifted painter as was his friend Mr Finglow, but who am I to pronounce? Strangely enough, one of his most frequent visitors, often to be found there when we call, is Mr Ralph Delaval, who was, in a way, the author of his misfortune, for it was Mr Delaval's imprudent and inconsiderate suggestion of pulling down the cottage to improve the view that led to the older man's illness and death. I believe Mr Delaval feels this a great deal, for he is very different in his manner from when he first came to Rosings; he is downcast and sober and does not rattle on as he was used to do. I think he would be glad to leave the neighbourhood, but seems incapable of making the decision to do so. The prime cause of the Delavals' lengthy visit – Miss Priscilla's ankle – must, by now, have been used up, though she still makes a great palaver about the pain the ankle gives her, and requires to be wheeled about in a basket-chair.

Charlotte says, and I do not entirely disagree, that Miss P. is setting her cap at Col. FitzWilliam, and that if he could get Miss Anne to cry off, she would have him before the cat could lick its ear. If that is so, I think the worse of the colonel – yet how can I judge? Miss Delaval has known him for some time. She told me she met him first in Derbyshire at the house of a Mr Bingley, where her brother was giving advice to Mr B. about improving his grounds. Miss P. gave me to understand that she quite lost her heart to the colonel on that occasion; and so persuaded her brother to travel into Kent at a time when she knew the colonel would be here, in hopes of meeting him again. Some parts of this tale are plainly true; yet it seems the Delavals must have contrived their accident so as to be invited within the gates of Rosings. I hardly know what to think . . . But I cannot like the air of artifice and machination that hangs over the business. Can there be any connection with the apparent disappearance of Lady Catherine? Surely not! There must be some quite different explanation for that. Her absence from home seems to leave the Delavals in a most equivocal situation, for no one at Rosings welcomes them, yet none can give them notice to go.

Meanwhile, I play my piano diligently and am practising some Beethoven sonatas which I hope to perform for you, dear Mrs Jennings, when I return through London. Mr Delaval was so kind as to procure them for me when he rode into Tunbridge Wells last week. He often comes and listens to me when I play the organ in Hunsford church (Mr Moss, the regular organist, is laid up with gout). Mr D. has said some very civil things about my playing, and he is a well-informed and clever man, so I value his praise (yet I cannot really like him).

Charlotte is of the opinion that, if Mr Delaval should make me an offer, I should accept him. She says that my chance of happiness would be as great as most people can expect on entering the state of matrimony. But what can she know about it? She is married to Mr Collins, who is tolerably good-natured, to be sure, but so prosy and self-satisfied that it is a penance to be together with him in a room for above five minutes. If Charlotte had not her children, her household and village affairs, her poultry and the advantage of interesting company at Rosings House, I do not know how she would tolerate her existence. Compared to Mr C., it is true, Mr D. is a positive paragon. And Charlotte insists that I should do my best possible to secure him. But, dear Mrs Jennings, *I do not love him*, and my heart instructs me that marriage without love is a sin against the Holy Ghost. Must I, then, remain unwed all my life? I wonder if I could ever support myself by my music? Charlotte says such an idea is quite ineligible, and yet – and yet!

Your affectionate friend,

Maria Lucas

PS Oh, dear, Mrs Jennings, how I *wish* that you were here to give me your cordial, fair-minded, unprejudiced advice!

IX

'Sir! *Sir!*' said Lady Catherine.

The bearded man stirred and snored, but offered no other reaction to her prodding and exhortations.

At this moment Lady Catherine almost fell into despair.

An uncountable, unmeasurable amount of time had passed, it seemed, since her first awakening in this rude habitation. Darkness had blanked out the two small windowpanes and then, later, daylight of a sort had come back again.

Meanwhile – a very frightening phenomenon – water had continued to penetrate under the door, pulsing in slowly but steadily in small rippling waves. A pool about the size of a card-table had collected, and more kept coming. This made Lady Catherine profoundly uneasy.

Suppose more and more came in, until it had filled the entire cabin? Was such a thing possible? Could enough water to *drown* her and the stranger flow under that door? More immediate and worrying was the likelihood that the incoming tide would submerge the man who lay on the floor, and put out the fire which Lady Catherine had with such difficulty persuaded to burn.

There was no means of preventing the water's entry – she considered laying her sable cloak against the crack, but immediately dismissed this expedient. The only remedy she could fix on was bailing. There was a shovel by the hearth, and a pail. With desperate energy, but no great skill, Lady Catherine scooped up water with the shovel and tossed it into the pail. When this was full, she emptied it down the drain hole. By such means, working at frantic speed, she managed to keep abreast of the water's inflow. The pool inside the door grew no larger. But it was punishing work for somebody wholly unaccustomed to physical labour. After two or three hours, however, she began to feel that the threat was diminishing; the ripples came more slowly, then they ceased. The pool inside the door gradually sank into the earth floor and left no more than a mud patch.

All this time the comatose stranger had not woken.

Lady Catherine leaned her aching back against the

wall and contemplated him. At this moment he shifted slightly and let out a grunt, or moan.

'Sir!' said Lady Catherine.

He made no reply.

With considerable reluctance, for she was as tired as she had ever been in her entire life, Lady Catherine knelt by him and introduced some spoonfuls of water, and then a dribble or two of apple pulp, between his yellow and battered teeth. She was mortally afraid of choking him, for he now began to struggle and groan, and received the nourishment without any sign of goodwill or gratitude, or without displaying any sign that it had benefited him.

Still he did not emerge into consciousness and now, exhausted and devoid of hope, Lady Catherine began to wonder if he ever would.

And then, suddenly, he opened his eyes.

They were large, grey and bloodshot, the whites dark yellow and threaded with red veins. He stared about him vacantly for several minutes. He was still lying on the mattress on the dirty floor, for there had been no means of hoisting him up into the hammock, and in any case, Lady Catherine wanted the hammock for herself. But she had covered him with her sable cloak and managed to insert the solid and bulky sable muff under his heavy head so as to reduce the danger of choking while she fed him.

His eyes roamed the interior vacantly for a moment or so, then came to rest, with utter amazement it seemed, on Lady Catherine, who had seated herself beside him on the three-legged stool.

'Who *are* you?' she demanded. 'Where are we? Who are you?'

He took a long time to consider this question.

His answer, when it came, terrified her.

'I am Azrael, the Angel of Death. That's who I am!'

Lord have mercy on me, thought Lady Catherine. I am locked up with a lunatic.

Only one thing about his answer reassured her in the least. He spoke with a rough, West Country accent, which, in the last few days of travel, she had become accustomed to hearing. This gave her, if nothing else, a feeling of location.

'Where are we? Where is this place? Who has shut us in?'

Accustomed to being furnished instantaneously with all the information she required, she spoke with all her accustomed sharpness of manner. But his answer came in a slow, pondering tone, and after a considerable pause.

'Where? Ay, that's a naggy one. In limbo, mayhap.'

Then he added, after a long, perplexed survey of Lady Catherine, in her draggled, drenched, crushed travel costume of silks and velvets:

'If I am Azrael, who must you be? One o' the Furies? One o' the Friendly Ones?'

'Speak sensibly!' said Lady Catherine. 'I am not accustomed to being answered with this kind of idle talk. Don't give me such flummery, but tell me who you are and where this place is. First – what is your name?'

He gave a deep sigh, a long, long exhalation, as if he were saying goodbye to some precious bubble of air, cherished inside his lungs, or some beloved dream which he had hoped to hold inside him for ever.

'Trelawny. Benjamin Trelawny.'

'How did we come to be here?' Lady Catherine asked, cheered by this sign of sense.

'Ah. I was on a ship. The *Sweet William*. From Santa Ana. She stove on a rock. All lost. All lost.'

He kept repeating 'All lost', as if to convince his hearer of the large number of people who had lost their lives. 'All crew. All lost. All passengers. All lost.'

'You had friends? Family?' she could not help asking.

'Wife. Little son Ben. Two daughters. Papers. Furnishings. *Poems*. All lost.'

He looked around the empty room as if still expecting to see the family, the furnishings, the children.

Something stirred in Lady Catherine's mind. I have never known a loss like that.

'When did this occur, sir?'

He shut his eyes and covered them with his hands.

'Time gone. They picked me up. Fishers. Picked up in sea.'

Plainly he would have liked to sink back into sleep, perhaps for ever, but Lady Catherine was determined to get more information out of him, no matter how ruthless she had to be in procuring it.

'Where is this place? Why are we here?'

'Brought in – harbour. Left with doctor. That's all. That's enough.'

'No, sir, it is *not* enough! I wish to know why I am here. Why we are imprisoned in this dismal, comfortless cell; why we are not released. Who is responsible for this incarceration?'

'Who is res— Oh, *send me patience*!'

He lay back on the mattress as if exhausted. From having been flushed, he had now turned deathly pale, and beads of sweat rolled off his brow. Alarmed, Lady Catherine administered the only remedy she had to hand – a spoonful of apple pulp.

His face twisted in disgust. His eyes, which had been resolutely shut, flew open again.

'What the deuce is this – gnat's piss?'

'*Sir!*'

Lady Catherine was outraged.

'You should be thankful for what you have. There was nothing else in the place.'

'Eggs out yonder. Outside.'

'But the door is locked.'

'Oh, ay. True. Quite true.'

Slowly, and, it appeared, with excruciating stiffness and pain, he hoisted himself to a sitting, then to a standing position. Lady Catherine could now see that he was unusually tall, well over six feet, and so haggard and emaciated that she wondered if he had been in prison or had suffered some debilitating illness.

The reason for his standing was now made evident: it was so that he could delve into his breeches' pockets. He did so, first in one, then in the other, and finally brought forth a key.

'Locked door – keep out thieves – meddlers—'

He lurched uncertainly to the door, thrust the key into the lock and turned it.

Lady Catherine was beside herself with wrath.

'Do you mean to tell me that all this time – *all this time* – if I had known, I could have been free, have left this miserable den?'

'Couldn't have gone far, though,' said the man. He leaned weakly against the wall and made a vague, fumbling gesture towards the vista beyond the doorway.

The noise of rushing water had grown considerably louder.

Lady Catherine stepped to the doorway and looked out.

Her spirits, which had risen a moment ago, sank sickeningly. She saw that the building which housed them stood on a point of rock between two overflowing water-courses. These met together beyond the point and poured into the ocean – white tumultuous waves hurling themselves ferociously on to a rocky coast.

'Can't get out till flood goes down. This is an island, now, see? Or as good as.'

The man, Ben Trelawny, turned indoors again and sat down on the mattress.

'Terrible floods they've been having in the West Country,' said Mrs Jenkinson. 'My sister writes from Bristol that rivers have been bursting their banks and tides have been extra high; my sister's letter has taken more than *ten days* to reach me. Do you think, Lord Luke, that it may be on account of these circumstances that we have heard no more relating to poor Lady Catherine? It is dreadfully worrying, indeed! One does not know what to think.'

'Yes, there may be something in that,' agreed Lord Luke quite cheerfully. 'I have been reading in *The Times* newspaper, which Mr Delaval was so kind as to bring me from Ashford, that the port of Brinmouth has been half washed away by the flooding of the Brin River bursting its banks and rushing down unexpectedly from the high moorland country farther inland, with great loss of life and many houses, and the harbour wall swept straight into the sea. Was not Brinmouth the port from which my sister proposed to take ship for the Great Morran?'

'Yes, indeed it was! Oh, gracious me! Poor Lady Catherine may be waiting to embark all this time at some wretched hostelry.'

'You think, then, Mrs Jenkinson, that the ransom note may be nothing but a hoax?'

'Oh, I do not know *what* to think!' exclaimed Mrs Jenkinson, bursting into tears. She clapped her hands to her brow, crying, 'My head! Oh, my poor head! This will be the death of me!' and tottered away to her own room.

'She has suffered from many more migraines since my mother left Rosings,' Anne remarked calmly. 'You would think it would be otherwise, considering the hard life she leads when Mamma is at home.'

'Perhaps she is one of those people who thrive best under a tyrannical rule,' suggested Miss Delaval.

'She is worried about what will happen if my mother never comes back,' said Anne.

'The boy Joss is here wishful to speak to you, my lord,' announced Frinton.

'Oh, bless me! I wonder if he has made any find of importance?' Lord Luke hoisted himself eagerly from his chair. 'I will see him in the library, Frinton,' and he hurried from the room.

'Wait, Uncle! I have something for Joss. I will come with you,' Anne said, following Lord Luke. She paused in the doorway and turned to cast a somewhat satirical glance at Miss Delaval and Colonel FitzWilliam before she went out, leaving them together.

Maria Lucas, after practising on the church organ for an hour, felt herself reluctant to quit the sequestered, tranquil little building. Dearly though she loved her small niece and nephew, she sometimes found their addiction to non-stop games highly fatiguing. Furthermore, now that their father was returned from Hertfordshire, no place in the parsonage was safe either from the children's wish to play, or their father's loquacity.

The organ in Hunsford church was located in a gallery over the main entrance, looking down on to the nave. When she had played her fill, Maria transferred to the bench that ran along by the gallery rail, tucked her feet on a hassock and rested her elbows on the rail, her chin on her arms, and brooded.

I ought to go home, she thought. This Kentish visit has lasted too long already. Meeting Colonel Fitzwilliam

again has unsettled me. I thought I would know, after being in his company again, whether I loved him or not; but I still am not sure. Seeing him troubles me deeply – but is that love? It causes me acute pain to see him in the company of Priscilla Delaval – but is that love, or mere despicable jealousy? I do not feel the same pain, or not to that degree, when he talks to Anne de Bourgh. Perhaps because their manner to each other is so cold and distant; or, because I know he marries her only out of compliance to family ordinance. But *does* he marry her? Is it merely a flirtation that he conducts with Miss Delaval, or has he indeed transferred his affections to her? Oh, how I long to be at home, soothed and fortified by familiar companions and duties . . . But Mrs Jennings writes that she is not in good health just now, and hopes that I can defer my return visit to Berkeley Street for a few weeks, since she wishes to see me again on my way home but has not, at the present time, sufficient strength to enjoy the shopping and the sociability that my visit would entail . . . Dear, dear Mrs Jennings, I hope there is nothing greatly amiss with her; she is such a kind, good friend . . . I am sure *I* do not wish for shopping and sociability, but merely to see her, and enjoy a comfortable talk with her, and listen to her advice. Charlotte gives me advice, and it is well meant, but it does not chime with my own sentiments. I think life with Mr Collins is changing Charlotte. I would not go so far as to say that it is making her hard-hearted, but she is not so accessible as she was to other people's feelings. She has to protect herself, I suppose.

Charlotte wishes me to remain at Hunsford until Lady Catherine's return, but when will that be? There is something decidedly odd regarding that whole business of Lady Catherine's visit to her sister-in-law. Can the woman be dead? Or gone away? It is not like Lady Catherine to be at the centre of a mystery . . .

Maria's head drooped more heavily on her crossed arms. The silence, the smell of damp stone, beeswax and aged woodwork calmed and lulled her, and she sank into a light repose.

She was wakened by the sound of voices – men's voices. They were not loud, but seemed quite close at hand. After a moment or two Maria realized that the two men in question must be standing just down below her, in the nave of the church.

'You have not heard from your uncle?'

'No, not since the original arrangement was made.'

'It is very disturbing . . .'

'There was to have been a second note?'

'Certainly. My uncle gave the first note to the maid, Hoskins, to be despatched from Launceston or Truro.

Then the second note should have been despatched from Brinmouth.'

'By which time the transfer to my uncle should have taken place and the – and the domicile established.'

'Just so. Is it not strange that you have heard nothing from your uncle?'

'Well – even at his best he is not communicative. I see no reason, simply from his silence, to conclude that the scheme has gone awry.'

'It is disturbing, though. My uncle is far from easy in his mind. He fears that something – something untoward, some mischance, may have taken place.'

'The whole affair – I collect such were to have been your uncle's intentions – was to have been merely a trick, a laughable artifice, nothing serious, a mere piece of foolery?'

'Of *course*!'

'Your uncle's aims in the matter being – not ransom?

'Dear me, no. His aim in the matter was – *don't* ask me why – some time for him to spend alone at Rosings, or at least without his sister's overbearing presence in the house, to search for something. Such a search as you have seen him daily concerned with. What his object is, he will by no means divulge – but to have my Aunt Catherine out of the way was to him a matter of prime importance. Connecting back, possibly, to some episode buried in the long-distant past when they were children together.'

'There was no financial incentive? I know that my uncle was paid a certain sum—'

'No such incentive was mentioned to me.'

While this exchange had been taking place, Maria was on tenterhooks.

Both voices were familiar to her. But by the time she had taken in the extraordinary, the outrageous nature of what was under discussion, it was too late to make her presence known. And in fact, she was too engrossed in listening, in trying to make sense of what they said, to wish to interrupt them.

'So what can be done?'

'Somebody should perhaps travel to the West Country to ascertain the state of affairs there.'

'Indeed yes, I agree, but who?'

'*You* are without doubt the properest person.'

'But I undertook to remain here.'

'Circumstances have altered, however.'

There was a longish pause. Then:

'They have indeed! The death of poor Finglow, for instance.'

Another pause. Then, coldly:

'What has that to say to anything?'

Maria decided that this had been going on long enough. She had brought a hymnal with her. She dropped this over the gallery rail and it fell into the nave with a loud thump.

There followed an appalled silence. Then a voice – that of FitzWilliam – called: 'Is anybody up there?'

Maria said, 'Yes.'

One set of hurried, running footsteps left the church. They sounded panic-stricken. After a moment slower, more measured steps could be heard mounting the stairs to the gallery.

Maria picked up her music and met Colonel Fitz-William at the top of the stairway.

X

Letters found in the attics of Rosings House

My dearest, dearest L.,
It is Christmas night. The snow is ticking against the window panes. I lie in my chilly bed, with B. beside me, and listen to the sobbing of the wind. I do not sob myself, but my heart is heavy – very heavy, at the knowledge that never, nevermore in this life shall I lie beside you, shall I be able to reach out my hand to touch yours, that although hardly a mile of parkland divides us, we are as severed as if the whole globe lay between us, as if you were in the Antipodes or the Indies. Your hand! I can feel it between mine as if it lay there in fondness and comfort, as it has so many, many times.

It is queer to recall that all our times of joy together were in spring and summer, with the song of birds and the scent of cowslips and may blossom around us – very different from tonight's hoary gloom and the ceaseless, relentless wind. We hardly knew how happy we were during that tender time. Oh, yes, we did; oh, yes, indeed, *indeed* we did.

I am not ungrateful. I *had* the time, and shall cherish the recollection of it until my dying hour.

I have risen from my couch and write these lines by the last glow of the embers. B. will not notice my absence from his side – he has this idea that abstinence from his connubial rights will shorten his time in purgatory and win him a swifter passage to paradise. You can believe that I am glad of this.

I have a Christmas gift for you, but it is not of the kind that can be tucked into our secret hollow in the old sycamore. No, you will have to wait until March or perhaps April to have knowledge of it.

Goodnight my love, my love. A happy Christmas to you. I shall see you across the church tomorrow,

L.

Dearest L.,

The snowdrops in the parsonage garden are just beginning to show their tips above the ground. I wonder if yours are showing in the cherry orchard? (I think our garden is more sheltered.) I remember the wonderful greenish-white

counterpane of snowdrops between the black cherry boles when you and I first met there. You said: 'Are you telling your fortune by counting cherry trees, Mrs Godwin?' And I was shy, not knowing how to reply.

Later you made up a nonsense rhyme:

> Tinker, tailor, soldier, sailor,
> Butcher, baker, collier, nailor,
> Lawyer, farmer, carter, whaler,
> Parson, mason, bosun, jailer
>   None of these
>   Her heart can please
> Only one, in the cherry grove
> Has power to capture Lucy's love.

By the time you made up that rhyme, the celandines and wood anemones were replacing the snowdrops, and our honey-time had begun . . . It makes me happy to remember.

As I walk abroad now, the village women are beginning to look at me in a friendly way and to wish me Godspeed. Your Christmas gift will perhaps arrive in time for Easter.

My love, my love,

L.

Dearest L.,

Now the daffodils, which yesterday were whipping in the gusty wind, making a brave show – now they are bent and shattered under sharp snow and slashing hail. May it not be so with my hopes. I walk heavy now, but my heart is joyful. My preparations are all made – I have a cradle, robes, shawls, caps and a most loving welcome ready for the reminder of our halcyon orchard days. B. has at last become aware of my condition – but it does not seem to cause him any wonder or dubiety or mistrust . . . He thinks it a gift from heaven (as do I), or that it must, somehow, have come about without his having been aware of the matter (which, you might say, is the case).

Do I wish for a boy, or a girl? I will not tempt Providence by expressing a wish . . .

This comes with all my love,

L.

My dearest, dearest L.,

Now my time will soon be here. After this week I do not think I shall be able to make my way to the hollow sycamore, so here is an end of our correspondence. And, should anything untoward happen, should this be my last letter, it comes only to express again my deep, undying love. You were right that our clandestine meetings must cease. They did not become us, they did not become our companions, our duties, our lives.

But the feelings remain, and leave a glow that will irradiate all the rest of our days.

Still yours, on the edge of the abyss,

L.

Entry on a scrap of paper found in Sir Lewis de Bourgh's diary

She was brought to bed of a boy on this 23rd day of April 18—. She did not survive the birth. The boy, christened Barnabas Joscelyn by Mr Godwin, was put out to nurse in the village. I did not see the child.

Entry on another scrap of paper in Sir Lewis de Bourgh's diary

My wife, distressed at an outbreak of typhus fever in the village, ordered little Eadred to be fetched home from the foster mother's cottage. I made enquiry of Godwin as to his infant, likewise fostered out, but he informed me, without any signs of distress or anxiety, that it was lost; that the wet-nurse, a woman named Smith, a connection of the Hurst family, had left the village with the hop-pickers when they returned to their winter quarters in London (or wherever they hail from), taking little Barney along with her, as it seems she had developed a great fondness for the child. Godwin seemed relieved to be quit of the charge, an obligation to pay for the child's maintenance. He is a strange man. Has he always suspected? Or known? Is he glad to be rid of it? I found myself greatly distressed by the discovery of this loss – the more so as little Eadred does not thrive – C. is terrified that he has caught the fever from the village children. She herself is again in a promising way, so cannot devote herself to the child as much as she might wish.

I am not well – my head aches; my heart aches – I think more than I should do of L.

Little Eadred has left this world. Poor child! I should feel more grief than I do; sadly, he took after his mother, and I found it hard to love him as I ought; he was too fond of his own way and paid little heed to others. I had always wished for a girl child, and cannot help hoping that C.'s next will be a child of the female sex.

Oh, if *that* child were not lost, how happy should I be!

I have taken the fever – I suppose from Eadred, or from my rambles about the village while making discreet enquiries about little B.J. I suppose I am come by my deserts. I did wrong by C. to marry her without love. And in my intrigue with L., I wronged both her and her husband, a harmless God-fearing man (though of a gloomy puritanical turn of mind).

I must try to put my affairs in order. My mind turns much on that child. How I wonder what has become of him.

* * *

'Have you read it through?' said Anne to Joss.

'Ay, and a right struggle it were. Why do he have to make his g's like p's and his s's like f's? I never in all my born days saw such a scrambly hand.'

'Never mind that! Don't you see what it means?'

'It means your dad and Mrs Godwin did what they ought not. And they got punished for it.'

'I don't see that. Lady Catherine got punished too – her child died. And she and that child hadn't done anything wrong. It's queer – I never felt sorry for my mother before, but now I think I do. My father sounds rather a selfish man.'

'Seems they should never ha' got married. Him and Lady Catherine.'

'But never mind that,' Anne said again. 'Don't you see what this means?'

'Well . . .' Joss said slowly, 'mebbe I do and mebbe I don't.'

'That little garden book your mother left you – with notes written in the margin – don't you see, it is the same handwriting as the writing in those four letters from L. She must have given the book to Mrs Smithy. *You* were that baby – Barnabas Joscelyn Godwin. The – the person that you believed to be your mother was really your foster mother. She took you off to London – perhaps when the money stopped coming from Mr Godwin. Or because she wanted to keep you. Mrs Smith, was that her name?'

'Ay,' said Joss, pondering. 'Petronella were her given name. Petronella Smith. She kept house for the old boy, Sir Felix, a-many years. And he learned me Latin and she learned me how to live by my wits. But she always did say, true enow, that I'd have good luck did I come back to Hunsford. Or, at least, find out a secret.'

Joss sighed, pulled up a long stalk of grass and chewed on the tender end, then added:

'But what good luck is there in finding out that I'm Mrs Lucy Godwin's bastard? I *loved* my mam – Petronella. She done her best for me. What do I know about this Mrs Lucy, except that she picked up her skirts for his lordship?'

'Poor thing,' said Anne, pulling out another stalk of grass. 'I feel sorry for her. She sounds as if she had a lonely life. But anyway, don't you see,' she repeated, 'it means that you and I have the same father!'

'Ay,' Joss slowly agreed, 'so it do . . .'

Lady Catherine had great difficulty in getting Ben Trelawny to converse. For several days he tended, from time to time, to return to his first premise and tell her that he was the Angel of Death and she an unclean spirit sent by Kismet to tempt him from the holy course of meditation that would, in the end, put him in contact with his lost loved ones.

'*I* have lost loved ones too!' said Lady Catherine irritably. 'You are not the only person who has had troubles in their life.'

But she was obliged to concede that to have lost a wife, three children, his entire fortune and an unpublished volume of verse which he had hoped that some English publisher would accept and bring out – all this greatly exceeded the loss of a son in his third year and a husband whom she had never valued above half.

But during one of Trelawny's rational periods, she persuaded him to take down the flitch of bacon and hack some slices off it. These, with eggs from the store hidden in a hole in the cliff outside, made a substantial difference to their diet.

Now that she had access to the environs of Trelawny's cabin, Lady Catherine realized that, though it was not precisely on an island, it might as well be until the flood subsided. The building abutted, on the point of a steep cliff, between two converging torrents, branches of the Brin River. There was no safe way across them as yet.

'Why do not people in the town come and rescue us?'

'Firstly, m'dear, they don't know we're here. And second, the poor souls likely got enough trouble themselves. There's a third branch of the river runs through the town. My guess is, if it's up as high as these, half the town is washed away.'

Halfway up the opposite cliff, caught in a tree, could be seen what Trelawny told Lady Catherine was the wreckage of her carriage.

He himself had been setting out to buy bread in Brinmouth village – 'It was afore the floods come down so bad, you could still cross by the stepping-stones' – when a crash from above made him look up, and he saw the coach come hurtling down the face of the cliff; a woman had been flung out and fell straight into the torrent, where she must have been swept out to sea. 'But she must ha' been dead already, falling from that height.' Trelawny himself had climbed up to the carriage, in which he found another female, deeply unconscious. 'There was no means of getting you back up on the road, m'dear, so I fetched a rope and lowered ye down.'

'You did all this by *yourself*? But could you not procure assistance from the village?'

'No time for that, lady. The Brin water was coming down powerful quick – as 'twas, I only just fetched ye into the cabin afore the flood had ris' up three feet, and there'd a' been no way of getting ye to dry land.'

'So you saved my life.'

'Didn' do so bravely then myself, did I?' said Trelawny with a wry grin. 'Reckon all that hoisting and dragging brought on a fit of the fever that struck me down after the wreck of the *Sweet William.* All I remember after that was lying on the floor and finding that somebody was dribbling sour-apple jam down my gullet. If it come to saving lives, ma'am, I reckon 'tis about quits betwixt us.'

And I probably saved you from drowning when the water came into the hut, also, Lady Catherine thought, but, contrary to her usual habit, she did not solicit praise for this.

'How long do you think it will be before the flood subsides?' she asked.

Three or four days at least, Trelawny guessed.

'You think no one will come in search of you?'

'Nay, poor souls. The Brin River comes down powerful heavy after a day's rain, and we've not had one day, but a whole fortnight – they'll have enow to do looking after theirselves. 'Sides, I'd left this cabin for a farm on the moor – only came back for a purpose I had.' He hesitated.

'Why *did* you dwell in this wild cabin, Trelawny?'

It had been many years since Lady Catherine had felt so much interest in another human being. But in such a small neighbourhood, comprising only one neighbour, it was only reasonable to avail oneself of what interest lay to hand.

'Well, ma'am, 'tis a story that, properly, is not all mine to tell. But, seeing as you was so solicitous as to fetch me back into this vale of tears' – he did not sound entirely grateful for this service, Lady Catherine noted – 'I've a notion I owe it ye. 'Twas like this, d'ye see . . .'

He stopped and scratched his white locks with a twig picked from the firewood pile, remarking, "'Tis to be hoped the water will go down before too many days, or it'll be cold comfort and raw vittles for us.'

'Proceed with your story, my good man.'

'Well,' he said. 'when I was fetched out of the sea after the wreck of the *Sweet William*, I lay like a corpse for a matter o' three weeks . . . I'd been carried to the doctor's house – there's a tolerable clever doctor in the town, Dr Lantyan – and when I began to speak and look about me and act like a human, he asked me if I'd any kin somewhere about the land who might pity my extremity and send me a few guineas. I told him of a nephew and niece in the north country, children of my dead sister, my only living connections. Whether they would come to my aid I did not know, for 'twas long enough since there'd been any word between us, but in the old days there was a kindness betwixt my sister and me. So Lantyan wrote them a letter, telling of my plight. Meantime I removed to this cabin, which was standing empty, for I'd been a charge on the doctor long enough. But a reply came, friendly enough, from my nephew, sending a sum sufficient to keep me for a few weeks. Being somewhat recovered by then, I wrote a grateful acknowledgement to him, and removed myself to a farm on the moor where I took lodgings. At this point, d'ye see, I began to take myself in hand.'

Trelawny stopped and looked hard at Lady Catherine.

'Did ye ever dream of me, ma'am?'

'Indeed no!' she replied, much astonished.

'Well, I've dreamed of ye, a-many times. 'Tis like this . . .' He paused and reflected for a moment or two. 'When I was lost in the sea, and all my loved ones lost, and all my goods and my fortune, not only that but the verses I had writ, those being the fruit of many years of contemplation – well, ma'am, 'twas like being stripped naked. And when I came back within myself after that calamitous loss and dispossession, I discovered a strange thing about myself. I found I had the power of foretelling events in my dreams. Some of them are trifling enough – a broken pot, a herd of cattle crossing the track, a sailor singing a shanty, a child picking a posy – but, time and again, I have dreamed of you, ma'am.'

'How singular. How very singular!' Lady Catherine spoke with disapproval. She did not care for the supernatural; one of her prime motives for the razing and demolition of Hunsford Castle had been the extirpation of its numerous ghosts. 'I wonder *why* you should do so?' Her tone of distaste suggested that his dreaming about her was an invasion of her privacy, which she felt to be unwarranted.

'That I cannot say, ma'am. I would not *choose* to do so – 'tis enforced upon me. But, anyways, living at this farm I began, as I say, to take myself in hand. I wrote, again, some of the verses I had lost. I wrote a memoir of my dear wife and children. I found a few pupils and taught them mathematics – I have always had a great partiality for algebra and geometry. Thus, I made enough to pay for my lodgings. And I dreamed a great deal and found comfort in my dreams – 'tis like hearing music playing in some faraway land – I feel the assurance that I shall see my loved ones again, not in this sphere but in some other . . .'

'But then,' said Lady Catherine, as he had again come to a halt, staring at the open door and the swollen river that rushed past it, 'but then, if you were safely and industriously established at the farm, and teaching mathematics' – her tone suggested that she found this a decidedly uncongenial and peculiar way to earn a living, but each to his own taste – 'why, what made you return to this dismal dwelling?'

'Ah, well, I was coming to that. I had a second letter from my nephew. He wrote to me that, if I were destitute, he had the means of assisting me to earn a sum of money. 'Twas in furtherance of a trick, a prank, a stratagem that was to be played upon a certain lady of his acquaintance – a certain Lady Catherine de Bourgh. She was to be waylaid, abducted, on her journey to visit a relative. She was to be kept confined for a certain period of time—'

'*What* are you telling me, sir?' ejaculated Lady Catherine, pale with wrath.

Maria Lucas, visiting Wormwood End with a pot of soup from the parsonage, found Anne de Bourgh there, arranging snowy boughs of cherry blossom in a copper jug.

'Oh, I interrupt you! I will not stop – I just came to bring this.'

Ambrose said, 'You are both of you more welcome than I can say. Do not think of leaving. Please stay and take a glass of cowslip wine.'

'No, don't go, Miss Lucas,' Anne gave Maria a friendly smile. 'Stay, and heat up your soup. Mr Mynges, you should heat it at once. You are growing so *thin* – I believe you have lost weight since I saw you last, and that was only two days ago.'

'Please, will you not call me Tom? I miss hearing that name used.'

'Tom, then.'

'Tom,' both girls said at the same time, and Anne asked, Where is Alice?'

'She spends very little time in the house. She misses

him. She is mostly to be found on the wooden bench under the plum tree where – he – used to sit at the end of the day . . .'

Young Tom's voice shook, and Maria laid a gentle hand on his shoulder.

'Look, here is your soup made hot. It is Charlotte's speciality – chicken and partridge with almonds and cream. Do try to take a little. She sends her very best regards, and would have come herself, but with the children, you know – and Mr Collins needs a great deal of attention just at present. He is in a state of utter desperation over Lady Catherine's absence.'

'Has anything more been heard about that?' asked Young Tom, obediently swallowing a spoonful of soup. 'It is a strange business indeed – strange and shocking.'

'You know, then, that my mother has been abducted?' Anne did not seem particularly surprised. 'I suppose the gossip is all over the village.'

'Ralph Delaval told me.'

Anne frowned. So did Maria, who said, 'What business was it of *his*? He had better have remained silent. It was not his affair.'

'I think,' said Young Tom, absently swallowing some more soup, 'he comes here driven by conscience. He feels such guilt and horror over – over Tom's death.'

'And so he ought,' said Anne sharply. 'Whatever he

says to the contrary, it was he who put into Mamma's head the notion of pulling down this cottage.'

'Nothing can atone for that,' agreed Maria sadly.

Ambrose looked attentively at the two girls.

'You are both very young,' he said. 'When we are young we think a great deal about revenge and atonement and one act cancelling out another. But life is not like that. One act will *never* cancel another. All we can do is to go on, taking the past with us, using it, if you like, as a fertilizer for the future. You, Miss Anne, with your delight in gardening – you should understand that.'

'People who do wrong ought to be punished,' said Anne firmly.

'Then which of us would escape?'

Maria said, 'Mr Mynges—'

'Tom, Tom!'

'Tom, then. When are you going to start painting again? What you have said applies to yourself. You are punishing yourself by not painting.'

There was a tap on the door, and Ralph Delaval put his head round it.

'Do I intrude?'

He was pale and grave, and appeared daunted at the sight of the girls, but Ambrose said:

'No, no, come in, come in. The young ladies are scolding me for my idleness.'

'Then I will come and sing the praises of inactivity and sloth. But please do not let me drive you away—' as the ladies rose to go.

'I promised my uncle I would help him sort some papers,' said Anne.

'I promised to take my niece and nephew for a walk,' said Maria.

When they were away from the cottage:

'Why *does* Delaval go there so much?' said Anne.

'Without any doubt, it is because he feels remorse over Mr Finglow's death. And I collect – he had some hand in your mother's abduction, which has somehow gone amiss.'

'How in the *world* do you know that?' Anne stopped and stared at the other girl in astonishment.

'I overheard a conversation.'

Maria told Anne what had occurred in the church.

'Then, after that, Colonel FitzWilliam came up the stairs and found me. I was unutterably shocked, as you can imagine. It has *completely* altered my opinion of him. And so I told him. How could he help to perpetrate such a plot! Not only he, but Lord Luke and the Delavals were involved. It is the most monstrous thing!'

'Well, I can understand my uncle,' said Anne, pondering. 'He has always been of a strange, whimsical, eccentric turn of mind. And he and my mother have always quarrelled. I think she did something dreadful to him when they were small. And I dare say he would consider it just a prank—'

'A prank!'

'I wonder what he is searching for? Some treasure, which he hopes to find in the attic before my mother returns?'

'But in the meantime, what has become of *her*?'

'I wonder how the Delavals came to be embroiled in the business?'

Maria said: 'Something she once told me suggested that she has formed a strong attachment to Colonel FitzWilliam. She met him in Derbyshire at the house of Mr Bingley. And any excuse would serve so that she might see him again.'

'She is welcome to him,' said Anne flatly.

'Ah, but Miss Anne, you forget – she has not got fifty thousand pounds!'

In the distance they saw Miss Delaval being propelled across the pleasure gardens by Colonel FitzWilliam. Miss Delaval waved her handkerchief, and the colonel bowed.

Both girls waved back coldly.

Joss had brought down from the attic a heavy, squarish object, rather larger than a portmanteau, swathed in layer upon layer of felt blankets and tied round and round

with innumerable cords. Both cords and blankets were stiff and greasy with encrusted dirt.

Lord Luke was beside himself with excitement. It was evident that the size and shape of this latest discovery filled him with the most eager expectation.

'The cords must be cut,' he said. 'But with great care, I beg.'

Joss produced a pruning knife, razor-sharp.

'It is like undoing a mummy,' said Anne. 'Let us hope there is not a curse attached to it.'

After carefully slicing through the cords, Joss unwrapped the overlapping stratifications of felt, dislodging from between them clouds of evil-smelling dust and rattling showers of dirt.

'Bats' droppings, likely!' he said with a grin.

'Ugh!' said Anne. 'Uncle Luke, if this is your treasure, I only hope it is going to be worth all the nastiness!'

'Oh, it is, it *is*!' cried Lord Luke in rapture. 'It *is* my lost desk!'

And indeed, what was revealed, as the last wrapping greasily unfolded itself, was a small writing-desk, about thirty-six inches square and a foot in depth, made of polished oak. Swathed so tightly in so many layers of felt, the wood had retained its polish and pale colour. Lord Luke ran his hands over it lovingly; he almost embraced it, then felt for a secret latch on the underside, which caused the lid to rise up. Inside were revealed pigeon-holes, drawers, a pen tray, but also, and evidently of far more importance to the owner, a mass of pages, tightly crammed in, smothered with tiny grey writing and drawings.

'My lost land!' cried Lord Luke in ecstasy. 'My lost land of Lassarto!'

'*Lassarto*, Uncle Luke? What in the world is that?'

'Oh, when I was a boy – between ten and fourteen – I imagined this land, its name was Lassarto. I wrote about it all the time, poems, stories – your mother at that time used to listen, she was fond, as enthusiastic about it as I was. Hours we used to spend, making up adventures for the Duke of Lassarto . . .'

With delicate care he selected one of the papers and read:

> 'Black were the clouds above the roof
> Where Ombla's chapel guards the pass
> 'Neath wicked skies the holy shrine
> Contends against the satanic force
> And ever in the eerie hush
> Fair Lydia bows her innocent head
> But will her prayer prevail? Alas!
> They lift aloft the accursed wine
> But will fair Lydia touch the glass?
> And will her fingers break the bread?'

'Good heavens, Uncle Luke!' said Anne. 'Did you write that?'

'Yes, when I was ten. By the time I had reached fourteen, my verses were far better than that. Just wait till I show you – till I find one . . .'

He began delving with trembling but meticulous fingers among the mass of papers, muttering to himself:

'But then I was sent off to Eton – oh, that nearly killed me! Then on the grand tour, and then with my Uncle Torvil to Bombay . . . And when I got back, Hunsford Castle was nothing but a pile of dust, and sister Catherine wed to her Sir Lewis, and swearing up hill and down dale that all the castle furnishing had been burned, discarded, given to the gypsies . . . Here, listen to this:

> 'Oh, hearken when by Nyla's bower
> The lovesick Indian maid
> Beguiles the melancholy hour
> With ditties softly played—'

I think I like the ten-year-old verses better,' said Anne, 'but oh, Uncle, good heavens, what hours of labour you put into it! I am not surprised that you wanted to retrieve it. I am very happy for you. Now you have got all you wanted, have you not?'

Anne's eyes met those of Joss, who was thoughtfully

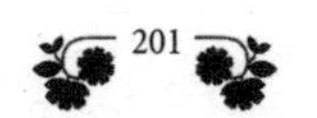

and methodically folding up the sheets of filthy felt and winding up the tangles of grimy rope.

'Yes, yes,' muttered Lord Luke, lovingly delving among his dusty manuscripts. 'Yes, yes. Joss, you shall have ten gold guineas.'

Anne said, 'Now had you not better apply your energies to rescuing my mother and bringing her home?'

'But I do not know where she is!' said Lord Luke.

Letter from Mrs Charlotte Palmer to Miss Maria Lucas

My dear Miss Lucas,

I'm as sorry to write you these sad tidings as you can't think, but truth must be told there's no way round it, and it's an ill bird that don't sing its song without roundaboutation, so to put it plainly, my dear mother Mrs Amelia Jennings is no more.

She succumbed to a catalepsy after celebrating our little Frederick's second birthday last week, which day we marked by a trip along the river and a dinner at Maidenhead, at which dear Mamma was so injudicious as to partake of fried cowheel and onion on top of a suet pudding. In two days she was no more, as I said, despite cupping and blistering and glistering. I thank Providence her sufferings were not of long duration, for they were dreadful. She lost the use of her right side, and it was a sad sight to see her who had used always to be so cheerful and fond of a good laugh and a well-served dish rendered so mute and mumchance. We shall miss her jokey ways inexpressibly and for years to come.

She spoke many times of you, dear Miss Maria, while she still had the use of her faculties, and told us often how she enjoyed your letters, which seemed, she often said, to display all the beauties of Kent before her. In token of her goodwill towards you she had sent for her lawyer last month and had him set down that she bequeathed you fifty thousand pounds in her will. (Don't think, dear Miss Lucas, that you are depriving Lady Middleton, my sister, and me, for Mamma had seen us amply provided for – our papa had left her very well established – and besides, our husbands are both comfortably placed. So we are pleased for you to have the money. At least I am. Lady Middleton bears the loss with Christian fortitude.)

Mamma has left me and Mr Palmer the house in Berkeley Street, so if you wish to stop with us on your return to Hertfordshire, only say the word and we shall be rejoiced to accommodate you. We shall be in town for some months yet, settling Mamma's affairs, and glad to have you with us at any time, to stay as long as you like.

Your sincere friend and well-wisher,

Charlotte Palmer

XI

Trevose Farm made a most acceptable change from the cabin between the two waterfalls. It was a large, rambling but solid edifice, situated in a dip on the headland above the port of Brinmouth. The town, far below, was hidden by the hill, but Lady Catherine, from her bedroom window, had a view of the sea, a blue, shimmering triangle, and liked it very well.

'If only I could contrive such a view of the sea from Rosings!' she sighed.

'How far off is it, ma'am?'

She was obliged to admit that the distance from Rosings to the sea was over thirty miles.

The farm was prosperous enough to employ about half a dozen people, who went placidly about their work and paid little heed to the two lodgers. Mrs Green the farmer's wife was willing to help Lady Catherine take a most welcome bath in a wooden tub of hot water, and pegged out her sable cloak to dry on a washing-line.

'Mid as well dry 'un afore brishing 'un with a besom brush, then that'll come up handsome,' she declared.

'Thank you, my good woman! I cannot pay you until I have written to my home for money,' Lady Catherine explained. 'All my cash was in a purse in the carriage which was lost.'

Mrs Green brushed this aside.

'Niver fret for that, m'dear – 'tes all one to us whether 'tes now or now-day month. You bide your time and don't 'ee trouble yourself.'

So Lady Catherine enjoyed the comfort of her big, peaceful bedroom – which had whitewashed walls and hardly any furniture, but was warmed by a driftwood fire – without anxiety, and spent much time there in the window seat, looking out at her segment of sea.

She had suggested to Trelawny that she might proffer her diamond ear-bobs to the Green family as a collateral, but he was strongly opposed to this notion.

'What the plague use would *diamonds* be to these people? You would only saddle them with the problem of how to dispose of the stones – and that they certainly could not do in Brinmouth as it is now desolate, destroyed. What folk there need is wood, bread and bricks, not diamonds. Good God, ma'am, what in the world possessed ye to travel abroad with that load of useless gewgaws? No doubt you consider yourself lucky that they were sewn into your muff.'

'I always travel with them,' said Lady Catherine placidly. 'And also, you see, I did not wholly trust that young man who is staying in my house. Your nephew, you say he is? Well, as you must already know, he is a decidedly ramshackle character. His zeal in promoting my plan to take this trip to the West Country seemed somewhat odd to me at the time – I wondered then if it could be my diamonds he was after. So I left the false ones behind, those I always keep for second-class occasions. Naturally, then, I had no inkling of this preposterous plot hatched between him and my brother and my nephew FitzWilliam – *prank*, forsooth! Well, they shall all feel the consequences in my will.'

Trelawny had told Lady Catherine how he was offered payment in a letter from Lord Luke to meet the coach in Brinmouth and transfer its drugged passenger to the Greens' farm, where she would be kept incommunicado for a week or so. But the scheme had fallen disastrously apart, with the accident to the coach and the death of Hoskins. What became of the coachman was unknown. He had presumably recovered consciousness at some point, and staggered on down into Brinmouth, where he may well have been swept away in the flood in which many others perished.

'Speaking of wills,' said Trelawny, who had walked down into the shattered town to see if there was a newspaper to be had and to visit his friend the doctor, 'talking of wills, ma'am, I must tell ye that your purposed visit to your sister the Duchess of Anglesea will be a waste of time – that is, if ye were still reckoning to make it? The duchess died five days ago. Dr Lantyan told me. I grieve to have to bring you this news.'

'Adelaide was not my sister, only my sister-in-law,' Lady Catherine calmly explained. 'Married to my brother James. *He* won't greatly grieve at her loss, I dare say. He is off in Spain, losing one regiment after another, by all accounts. And Adelaide, a most difficult, cantankerous woman, had chosen to immure herself down at Great Morran. Well, I only hope that she has not made a shockingly injudicious will. The prime object of my visit was, if possible, to prevent such an outcome. She had an immense fortune settled on her by her own father – I trust she has not left it all to a home for superannuated female harpists.'

'No, not that. I was going to tell ye: her attorney told Lantyan that she has left a large portion of her fortune to a nephew, Granville FitzWilliam.'

'Oh,' said Lady Catherine very thoughtfully, '*has* she,

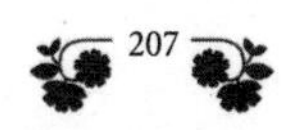

indeed? I fear that will materially reduce my daughter Anne's chance of getting married. Without the inducement of a fortune, there will be little hope of persuading FitzWilliam – good-natured and obliging though he is – to take the wretched girl. Nor am I sure that I would wish him to. This disgraceful affair has materially lowered him in my estimation. Does your friend the doctor have any information as to when the funeral will be held, and where?'

'Yes, ma'am. It will be at the duke's principal home in Somerset, Zoyland Abbey, in ten days or so, when he has returned from the peninsula.'

'Then,' said Lady Catherine, sighing, 'I had best bestir myself, now that you and I are both on the mend, and write home for some money and clothes suitable for the obsequies. Heigh-ho! It has been so pleasant staying here, free from care; I have enjoyed my conversations with you, my good friend. How disconcerted they will be, at home, to know that I am still in the land of the living. And you, how glad you will be to resume your peaceful solitary existence of meditation and recollection.'

'Not entirely, ma'am. I too have valued our exchanges. When, if ever, I bring out my volume of recollections and recaptured verses, I should like, if you have no objection, to take the liberty of dedicating it to you.'

'Certainly. I shall be gratified – honoured, indeed.'

Surreptitiously, Lady Catherine touched her eyes with a handkerchief.

Letter from Lady Catherine de Bourgh to Miss Pronkum

Trevose Farm, Brinton, Cornwall

My good Pronkum,
My present direction is this farm, which lies due south of the port of Brinmouth. Pray bring me clothes suitable for a funeral (my black satin, the jet-trimmed turban, the black mantilla, etc.), besides one or two walking costumes and two or three evening gowns. Also a hundred pounds in ready cash. Do not attempt to pass through Brinmouth town, which has suffered severely from flooding, but take the back roads from Truro. I shall be attending the Duchess of Anglesea's funeral at Zoyland some time next week. You may inform Lord Luke and Col. FitzWilliam that I have met Mr Delaval's uncle, Mr Trelawny. After the funeral I shall return to Kent.

Catherine de Bourgh

Maria was playing to herself on the organ of Hunsford church. More and more often, latterly, she had availed herself of this solitary distraction. The atmosphere at the parsonage, these days, was anxious and fretful; and at

Wormwood End she was almost always liable to encounter Mr Delaval. 'I do not greatly care for Mr D.,' she had written to Mrs Jennings, and she had not since then found any particular reason to alter that opinion. Oh, dear, dear Mrs Jennings, how very much I miss you, thought Maria, playing a mournful air by Gluck. Writing to you seemed to clarify my thoughts. And the prevailing mood up at Rosings House was strange indeed. Still no news of Lady Catherine; the colonel plainly deeply worried; Lord Luke utterly absorbed in some document he had discovered with the help of Joss and Anne de Bourgh. Anne herself, who had hitherto appeared to despise her uncle and hold him at a very low estimate, had now completely changed her attitude and seemed to regard Lord Luke with a kind of amused affectionate awe, As one might, thought Maria, regard a sparrow that suddenly began to chirp out the sonnets of Shakespeare.

Sighing, Maria shuffled her music together and prepared to return to the parsonage.

In the church porch she found Colonel FitzWilliam.

She had intended to pass him by with a cool and brief 'Good morning', but he detained her.

'Miss Lucas – Miss Maria—'

His tone was humble, almost supplicating.

'What is it, Colonel FitzWilliam?'

It was not in the nature of Maria Lucas to be unkind. The gentleness of her voice could be interpreted as solicitude and goodwill, and Colonel FitzWilliam did so interpret it. He said:

'Miss Lucas, my dearest Maria – for dearest you must always be to me, despite all the wrong and tragic events that have fallen in our way – during these last weeks I have come to understand more and more clearly how sorely I need you. I have come to believe that I cannot do without you. Deep and bitter conviction makes me tell you this. I know that I have not the shadow of a right to claim your goodwill, but my need for you overrides my duty to others, my awareness of the wrong I have done to others. I am not a bad man, Miss Maria, I believe I have it in me to be a good one, if you were by my side. If you would only accept and guide me, I believe it would lead to great happiness for both of us. We – we should not have very much to live on, but now, I believe, that is of little importance.'

He looked at her beseechingly.

Maria took a long, deep breath. Then she said:

'Colonel FitzWilliam, you truly astound me. What of your duty to Miss Anne de Bourgh? Are you not promised to her?'

'Yes, yes,' he said impatiently, 'but that is only a packthread tie, the merest breath would break it. I will not malign my cousin Anne at this time, but I believe she has plans of her own which do not include me.'

'This puzzles and shocks me more than a little, Colonel, for I have not been able to help observing that, though betrothed to your cousin, you have been paying what seemed unmistakable attentions to another lady, Miss Delaval.'

He flushed and said shortly, 'You must also have observed that Miss Delaval is the sort of woman who expects as her right those little attentions, encouragements and services which mean nothing to both parties, but are merely the regular material of social dealing. Anybody who reads more than *that* into my relation with Miss Delaval makes a grievous mistake.'

'I think *you* make a mistake there, Colonel FitzWilliam. I think the lady has read a great deal more into your connection with her than you admit; I think what you call the regular material of social dealing may have led to harm and mischief. As—' Maria stopped and swallowed.

Colonel FitzWilliam broke in.

'No, no, there I am sure you are wrong. I am sure, I – I hope so. Miss Delaval is a well-bred, accomplished, easy-spoken lady who has been about the world and does not – does not wear her heart on her sleeve. I am sure you are wrong,' he repeated eagerly.

'But that is not the end of what I have to say, Colonel,' Maria doggedly continued.

'Remember last summer!' he pleaded.

'I do remember it.' Involuntarily Maria laid a hand upon her heart as if to quiet a sudden pang. 'I did love you then. I do not deny it. But – we grow, and we change, Colonel. I have grown, I think. And I have changed. I looked up to you last summer; I did not know you as well then as I know you now. Events have taken place – strange, dreadful things have happened. They may have changed you. They have certainly changed me. I fear I do not feel towards you now as I did then. I – I have different plans. I—'

She swallowed, thinking of Mrs Jennings's legacy, about which she had told nobody. What would the colonel say if he knew of that? Would he back away in horror, believing that she took him for a fortune-hunter? She could almost have laughed, looking up at his melancholy, hangdog, craggy face.

'I am sorry,' she said flatly. 'But there is no future for us together, Colonel FitzWilliam. And I think there is no more to be said on this subject. So – I bid you goodbye!'

She turned, and almost ran across the churchyard.

Did I do right, Mrs Jennings? 'Now *don't*,' Mrs Jennings had urged her, 'don't you go into Kent thinking you've got to find a husband there. I want you so to have a husband, as you can't think, but it's not got to be just any husband, mind! Both my girls have got decent, good men they can rely on, and that's what I want for you, my dearie! So don't you take the first that offers, if he don't suit, but come you back and stay a month or two with me in London and look about you, and first and foremost, *don't be in a hurry*! There's plenty fish in the sea. Besides which, there's more things in a girl's life than husbands. There's your music, for instance. Remember a husband is not the be-all and end-all.'

Which is certainly true, thought Maria, considering her sister Charlotte, who had her children, her house, her garden, her poultry – and Mr Collins.

Her recollection of Mr Collins was perhaps prompted by the sight of Mr Collins himself, red-faced and panting, hastening at a highly incautious pace along the lane that skirted Rosings Park between the mansion and the parsonage.

'News, great news!' he shouted as soon as he saw Maria. 'Most prodigious, most excellent news! Lady Catherine has been heard from at last! And she will soon be on her way home!'

Anne had persuaded her Uncle Luke out into the little fountain courtyard, where he was pacing to and fro, reciting his 'Ode to Orpheus':

'When Orpheus plays upon his lyre
Seated beside his snowy fire
Where the clear, pear-shaped flames arise
To meet the dark and starry skies
And frosty sparkles deck the trees
And all the tumbling torrents freeze,
A troop of skipping colonels dance
With many a neat and sprightly prance
Kicking the snow in misty flurry
Each thinking of his dish of curry
Bald heads and glistening eyebrows white
On each moustache a stalactite . . .'

'Oh, Uncle Luke, I do love it. It is so preposterous! What made you *think* of these things?'

'They just tumbled out, my dear. Like the torrents. Of course, everybody I showed them to told me they were sad stuff. Even your dear mother was quite captivated by them at first, but then after I was sent off to Eton – I went to school very late, you know, because I was of a delicate constitution, my old trouble, you know – Catherine and I became, as it were, separated. She learned to despise my Lassarto "plays" as we called them; she condemned them as childish rubbish.' He rubbed his eyes. 'There was a shocking scene . . . for me, that was a grievous wound. I felt betrayed; but also I lost confidence in my own imaginings. It is a terrible thing to despise yourself,' Lord Luke said thoughtfully. 'I did that for many years. And then, up there in Wensleydale, I do not know how or why – perhaps it was the conversation of young Delaval, whom I met at Bingley's house—'

'*Delaval?*' Anne's voice was full of disgust and astonishment.

'Oh, I know, my dear. He is a sadly flibbertigibbet young fellow, there's no denying that. But then, so am I! But he has a lively mind, a lively, exploring questing mind, especially when he has taken a glass or two – I dare say he has never put forth his whole intelligence, displayed his real wit to you.'

'Indeed he has not! He considers me a boring little dowd.'

'Ah, pity, pity . . . He is a man for other men, it seems, not for females. Well, as I said, up there at Wensleydale I began to hanker more and more for my lost writings. I felt – foolish as it may seem to you – that if only I could be reunited with them, it might, as it were, open that vein again, touch off the hidden spring, make me a new start. I knew Catherine would never allow me access to them – supposing she even knew where they were, if they were even *there.* No: my only recourse was to go about my scheme by stealth. And only see how successful *that* has proved!'

He beamed at Anne triumphantly.

She had not the heart to point out that his successful scheme had resulted in considerable harm to other people. Besides, she was thinking of herself.

She said, 'Yes, you were hardly treated, Uncle. As Mamma treats most people. But at least you were allowed an education. But I – I have nothing at all. Nothing! My mother considered that I was not worth the trouble and expense. All I acquired were polite manners and a straight back.'

'Education?' he said wonderingly. 'You want an education?'

'Even Maria Lucas knows more than I do. She can speak French and play the piano. But the whole world of books and learning is closed to me.'

'Take care, my dear! Nobody loves a *femme savante*. But I dare say once you are married, supposing that you have an accommodating husband, you may perhaps be able to explore that world to some degree; learn French perhaps, read a few books. (It is true, there are not many books at Rosings.) Your father, dear fellow, was more of an outdoor man, as I recall, fond of birds and flowers and horses.'

'Oh, what was he like?' she cried inquisitively.

'Sweet-natured. Not as clever or strong-minded as your mother. He was ductile – easily led. She married him when he was very young – hooked him,' said Lord Luke with the ghost of a chuckle. 'He was very rich, of course. Old Sir Laurence de Bourgh had made a fortune from the manufacture of some garment. It was not referred to.' Another chuckle. 'No, my dear, 'tis true: if you want an education, you will certainly not find it at Rosings.'

He wandered over to the fountain, declaiming:

> 'It was upon a starlit, witching land
> Far, far beyond the creamy ocean's rim . . .'

At this moment a blood-flecked, muddy, dishevelled dog cantered, limping, into the walled enclosure. Unhesitatingly, though with a visible effort, it jumped up into the lowest basin of the fountain, and proceeded to roll and splash and lave itself, gulping thirstily at the same time from the descending spouts of water.

'Good heavens!' exclaimed Lord Luke starting backwards, decidedly put out, as he had been vigorously splashed. 'Where in heaven's name did that beast come from? Be off, sir! I do not care for dogs – never have done so.'

But Anne cried, 'Pluto! Dear Pluto! It is *Pluto*!'

She ran forward and flung her arms round the soaking, filthy animal. 'Oh, I am so happy to see you! Oh, just wait till I tell Joss!'

Lord Luke wandered away, shaking his head, murmuring: 'She wants an education. Now, why? What good has all that education ever done me?'

Priscilla Delaval said to her brother: 'We had best be away from here before Lady Catherine comes home. She seems, oddly enough, to have established the most cordial and favourable relations with our Uncle Ben – by who knows what singular process! But it seems inevitable that the whole silly scheme has been disclosed to her, and our part in it; we cannot expect to be *persona grata* at Rosings.'

Miss Delaval looked unwontedly low-spirited, almost haggard. Her mouth, normally curved into a half-smile, was turned down at the corners; a frown creased her brow, and her bright dark eyes held a hard expression. No dimples were to be seen.

Ralph said: 'Have the carriage by all means, my dear. It has been mended these three weeks and more. But I remain here. I must chance Lady Catherine's wrath.'

'You remain?' She was astonished. 'At Rosings? But why? What can be your object? There can be no chance of the diamonds *now*. Uncle Ben more or less intimated that Lady Catherine had suspicions of us – that was why she took them with her. What can you possibly mean to do?'

'I do not remain at Rosings. I plan to remove to Wormwood End.'

'*Wormwood End?*'

'Ambrose Mynges has invited me to take up residence with him in the cottage.'

Priscilla was speechless for many minutes, and could only stare at her brother in utter dismay and chagrin. Then she said:

'You must be mad. What will people say?'

'What they say will not affect me in the least,' he answered calmly.

'But – do you *like* Mynges?'

'Yes,' he replied shortly.

'What will you do with yourself?'

'Persuade him to start painting again. Take over the cooking. Advise a few of the local gentry about their parks.'

'But what about *me*? What shall *I* do?'

'Whatever you please.' He was not very interested. 'Marry FitzWilliam, if you have any sense.'

'But we know he is in Dun territory. And, even if he were not, he makes it plain—'

She stopped and bit her lip.

Ralph said, 'That is not so. Sneyd writes to me that FitzWilliam's aunt, the duchess, has just died leaving Fitz a fortune which will make him as rich as Croesus. Sneyd always knows this kind of thing before the rest of the world. Fitz may not even know this himself yet; but, take my word, it is so. You have only to put out your hand and draw him in.'

She said, 'That is by no means so easy as you seem to think.'

But a look of determination began to grow in her dark eyes.

XII

Anne and Maria were taking the children, Lucy and Sam, for a walk by the rushing stream where once Anne had seen the cat Alice apparently marooned on a rock.

'If they fall in you must promise to rescue them,' said Anne, 'for I can't swim.'

'Luckily,' said Maria, 'having four brothers, I swim like a fish. We used to go off on secret bathing expeditions in the Mimram River. My mother never knew!' She laughed, remembering. 'I used to swim in my shift. And once I was caught in reeds and nearly drowned. My brother Henry rescued me just in time, and they had to beat the water out of me.'

'How lucky you are, to have brothers. Darcy and FitzWilliam did not visit often enough for us to do things like that.'

'Tell a story, Miss Anne!' beseeched the children, when they had been inducted through the cave under the waterfall with many shrieks and giggles. 'Tell one of your stories! Tell about the cat Alice, and how she flew across the water on a magic carpet.'

'No, I will tell an even more exciting story about the dog Pluto. Once, the Wicked Queen said he must be drowned.'

'Why? Why? Why must he be drowned?'

'Because the Queen said he left messes on the clean grass. But that was not true.'

'Who had left the messes?'

'A badger, who came at night.'

'We know about badgers,' said Sam. 'We hear them grunting at night outside our window.'

'So poor Pluto was to be drowned. The Wicked Queen told two men called Muddle and Verity to tie a stone round his neck and throw him in the lake.'

'We know Muddle and Verity! They bring baskets of turnips and parsnips to the back door, and Mrs Denny gives them a glass of beer.'

'Muddle and Verity took the dog Pluto. But they were kind men so they did not drown him. They knew he was a very clever dog.'

'Why? Why was he clever?'

'Before he belonged to Joss, he belonged to a pick-pocket.'

'What is a pickpocket?'

'A wicked person who steals money out of other people's pockets. There are no pickpockets in Hunsford. But this was in London, where there are many people and many pickpockets. The one who owned Pluto was a boy called Prigfambles. He was very clever at slipping things out of pockets, and his dog Pluto was clever too. If there was a watch, or a gold guinea in a man's pocket, Pluto would sniff it out, and he would point with his nose to that pocket, and then Prigfambles would snatch it out, quick as lightning.'

'What happened to Prigfambles? Did he go to prison?'

'No, he got taken up by the Press Gang.'

'What's the Press Gang?'

'They take boys and men who are walking near the sea, and make them go on board ships to become sailors in the navy and fight for their country. So Prigfambles was taken for a sailor. And poor Pluto was very sad.'

'What happened then?'

'Joss found him and looked after him. So he loved Joss very much.'

'Did Joss ever pick any pockets?'

'Certainly not! All Joss wanted was to be a gardener.'

'What happened when Muddle and Verity took Pluto?'

'They had to go to Rochester to get some plants for the Wicked Queen that had been sent over from Holland. So they reckoned that, as Rochester was a long way off, if they took Pluto there in the gig, he would never find his way home but would probably look after himself well enough.'

'By picking pockets?'

'Perhaps! Or just by picking up scraps of food. So they took him to Rochester and left him there.'

'What did Pluto do?'

'He didn't stop one minute in Rochester, but looked about him and started on the long walk home.'

'How long?'

'Thirty miles. And he had to swim across rivers and climb hills and go across turnpike roads and – and fields with bulls in them, and go by farms where there might be farmers with guns and guard dogs who would try to fight him. So it took poor Pluto a long, long time to get back to Hunsford. Days and days and days.'

'What did he do when he got back?'

'You tell me!'

'He jumped right in the fountain and had a good wash!' chorused the children.

'Right! And then Joss came and gave Pluto a big dinner of rabbit stew and he slept for eight hours.'

'That is a good story. Now tell one of your Uncle Luke's stories about the Duke of Lassarto.'

'Once upon a time,' Anne began, 'the duke was riding on a horse all made of cloud.'

'Black cloud or white?'

'Black cloud, all black. It had eyes that were stars and reins made of rainbow. And its tail stretched right across the sky . . .'

'Go on, go on!'

It rained as hard on the day of Lady Catherine's return as it had on the day of her departure for Great Morran.

When the coach drew up on the gravel sweep, Frinton was waiting to throw open the house doors, while Muddle and Verity, Smirke and the boy Joss were assembled on the steps with umbrellas, to shield their mistress and Pronkum from the rain and to carry in the baggage. The dog Pluto, who, since his return, refused to be parted from Joss by more than ten yards, concealed himself under the coach as soon as it rolled to a halt.

'Welcome, welcome, your ladyship!' said Frinton. 'You are looking very well, if I may say so!'

Ignoring this, Lady Catherine glanced about her with a touch of her old discontent.

'Where is everybody?' she demanded. 'Oh, I suppose they are inside,' and she ascended the steps. Pronkum followed her closely, carrying a dressing-bag and a small bundle wrapped in striped satin.

Once inside the main entrance hall, Lady Catherine gazed about her a second time in dignified surprise.

'Where is everybody?' she asked again.

The Collinses were there, with Maria. And Lord Luke was there, wearing an anxious expression.

'Where is my nephew FitzWilliam? Where is Anne? Where is Mrs Jenkinson? Where are the Delavals?'

'We are so *rejoiced* to see you back, dear Lady Catherine,' hastily began Mr Collins with a whole series of bows, and Lord Luke said:

'I have to tell you, Catherine—' when suddenly the maid Pronkum let out a piercing shriek.

'My lady's diamonds! Where are they? They've gone!'

'Nonsense, Pronkum! What can you mean?'

'They were just here! I laid 'em on this marble table – and I went out to the carriage to get my lady's cloak-bag – and when I come back, they was gone! Gone! Just clean gone!' And she burst into hysterical laughter.

'No, really, this is too much!' exclaimed Lord Luke angrily. 'Those wretched diamonds are nothing but trouble. I wish to heaven, Catherine, that you had never acquired them! Let a search be made. They have probably been knocked to the floor by one of the fellows bringing in the bags.'

A diligent search was conducted, in and around the coach, up the front steps, throughout the entrance hall, in and behind the marble furnishings and statuary. No diamonds were forthcoming.

Then Joss said:

'Look at the dog.'

For Pluto, contravening all prohibition, had followed Joss in and glided like a black-and-white fish among the legs and skirts of searchers.

Pluto was standing beside Smirke and had his nose raised, like a pointer, towards the tails of Smirke's rusty black jacket.

'We'll just take a look in those tail pockets, Smirke,' said Lord Luke with unusual sharpness and decision.

'Oh, *sir*! You can't mean—'

'Take a look, Muddle and Verity.'

Briskly, despite Smirke's protests, the two men did so, and drew forth the striped satin bundle.

Pronkum had hysterics all over again.

'Oh, the *wretch*! Oh, how could you, you monster!'

'You had best call the constables, Frinton,' said Lord Luke wearily.

'Yes, my lord,' agreed Frinton, deeply shocked. But Smirke made a sudden dash and ran out through the open doors into the driving rain.

Joss said, 'I'm wholly sorry the dog came in, your

ladyship; but anyhow, seems he made hisself useful to ye at the last. I'm here to give in my notice, my lady, and say goodbye, for I'm off to – to stay with relatives in Wales.'

He ducked his curly head and nipped out between the double front doors almost as fast as Smirke had done.

'Dear me!' said Lady Catherine. 'Garden-boys giving notice? What next? What are things coming to? This is most singular – most irregular!'

'Best come into the saloon and sit down, Catherine,' said Lord Luke. 'For there is much to tell you.'

'But first,' said Charlotte Collins, 'let me take your hat and pelisse, my lady, and I feel sure you are in need of a little refreshment.'

Her tone was anxious, solicitous. It held a touch of commiseration.

'Where, pray, is Mrs Jenkinson?'

'I am afraid she has left your service, Lady Catherine.'

'*Gone?* But why? And where?'

'She – she began to feel her age. Those headaches from which she suffered so—'

'Headaches?'

'She sent you her humble apologies, my lady. She will be writing a letter of more complete explanation and apology as soon as she is settled.'

'Settled? But where? Where has she gone?'

Charlotte said, 'She has gone to live with relatives in

Wales. Will you not sit down?' Lady Catherine sat down in the saloon as suggested. A tray with wine and rout-cakes was put beside her. She sipped a little wine and her bewildered gaze swept round the room.

On the mantelpiece opposite her was a large portrait of Anne, life-size, sitting with a cat on her lap. One corner of it was unfinished.

'How did *that* get here? Where did it come from?'

'I imagine you recognize the style, Catherine,' said Lord Luke. 'It was by Desmond Finglow. His last picture. Anne has left it for you.'

'*Left* it? What can you mean? Where *is* Anne?'

'She has left a letter for you,' said Lord Luke. 'Here it is.'

Lady Catherine read:

My dear mother,

But the time you read this, I shall be in Wales, living with Mrs Jenkinson in the cottage that my father bequeathed in a codicil to his eldest child. But I am not that child. The person who owns the cottage is Joscelyn Godwin, who was my father's daughter by Mrs Godwin. She was brought up as a boy by the wet-nurse Petronella Smith, because the pay was higher for boys at nurse; and Petronella loved Joss and carried her off to London. When Joss grew old enough to choose, she could see very well that boys can make their way in the world more easily than girls. But she and I love each other like dear sisters, as we are, and we are going to share the cottage in Wales that my father left Joss, and Mrs Jenkinson is going to keep house for us. You will have to find another companion.

I am sorry to hear from Uncle Luke that you have been having a hard time of it in the West Country. But I hope you are now safe home.

Yours etc.,

Anne de Bourgh

It took Lady Catherine many minutes to assimilate the contents of this letter. Under Maria's pitying gaze, she seemed to age visibly as she read and thought about it.

She murmured, 'Joss? The *garden*-boy?' in tones of incredulity.

'Did you know about this?' she asked Luke. He shook his head.

'Not until latterly.'

He thought of Anne's ecstatic programme, which she had divulged to him.

'We shall get up at six. We shall read Latin – Joss knows it, old Sir Felix taught him – for two hours. Then breakfast. Then literature and French until twelve o'clock. Then we shall work in our garden. We shall have just enough money to live on, if Mamma continues to pay my allowance until my majority. If not, we shall sell produce from our garden. Joss says we shall be able to manage. It was kind of you to give Joss that ten gold guineas. We shall be able to live on that for some months.'

'Where are the Delavals?' Lady Catherine asked, as if she needed a respite from thinking about Anne.

'Ralph has gone to live with Young Tom.'

'Young Tom, who is Young Tom?'

'Ambrose Mynges, the younger of the two painters.'

'How very strange . . . And his sister? Miss Delaval?'

'She has returned to her home in Wensleydale.'

'I thought she planned to visit an aunt in Exeter? Or was that a lie? There have been so many lies told, I begin to feel quite confused. And FitzWilliam? Where is he?'

'He has returned to Derbyshire. He sent his best wishes and respects.'

'Ha! I know what value to put on *them*. That minx will get him. As soon as she knows about Adelaide's legacy, he is doomed . . . He would have been far better off with little Miss Lucas,' Lady Catherine said, half to herself, forgetting that the Miss Lucas in question was standing close beside her.

Maria said, in a gentle tone:

'Lady Catherine, would you like it if, for a while, I came here to Rosings to take over Mrs Jenkinson's duties? I am a famous housekeeper, I can promise you –

Charlotte will attest to that! When our mother was laid up with the pleurisy, I took over all the duties of the house till she was better, and that was a family of thirteen! And I would not be a stranger to your ways. What do you say? Shall I try for a while?'

Lady Catherine stood up shakily.

'Yes, thank you, Miss Lucas, I think that is an excellent suggestion. We – we shall talk again later. Now, if you will excuse me, I think I shall retire to my room for a while . . . So much to think about. Lucius!' She turned suddenly to her brother. 'I have many things to say to you!'

He quailed a little.

'Yes, Catherine.'

'But they shall not be said now. You—' Suddenly she sounded anxious. '*You* are not going off immediately – not going back to Derbyshire, not just yet, are you?'

'No, Catherine. Not in the immediate future. Not if I can be of any use here.'

'Good. I am glad to hear that. I shall come down again in a little while. Then I shall have a bone to pick with you!'

Lady Catherine left the saloon, with Charlotte and Maria following solicitously in her wake.

Lord Luke murmured, 'At the marriage banquets of the Sicilian poor, the bride's father, after the meal, is accustomed to hand the bridegroom a bone, saying, "Pick this bone; for you have taken in hand a much harder task . . ." Deucalion, after the deluge, was told to cast behind him the bones of his mother . . . To make no bones of a thing is the equivalent of the French "*flater le dé . . .*" '